CRYPTID FRONTIER

GERRY GRIFFITHS

SEVERED PRESS
HOBART TASMANIA

CRYPTID FRONTIER

WWW.SEVEREDPRESS.COM

ISBN: 978-1-922551-51-1

ALSO BY GERRY GRIFFITHS

DEATH CRAWLERS SERIES
DEATH CRAWLERS (BOOK 1)
DEEP IN THE JUNGLE (BOOK 2)
THE NEXT WORLD (BOOK 3)
BATTLEGROUND EARTH (BOOK 4)

CRYPTID ZOO SERIES
CRYPTID ZOO (BOOK 1)
CRYPTID COUNTRY (BOOK 2)
CRYPTID ISLAND (BOOK 3)
CRYPTID CIRCUS (BOOK 4)
CRYPTID NATION (BOOK 5)
CRYPTID KINGDOM (BOOK 6)

STAND-ALONE NOVELS
SILURID
THE BEASTS OF STONECLAD MOUNTAIN
DOWN FROM BEAST MOUNTAIN
TERROR MOUNTAIN

DEDICATION

You endured the orphanage,
Survived the blitz, and came to America
We miss you Mom

CRYPTID FRONTIER

(CRYPTID ZOO BOOK 7)

PART ONE

BLOOD IN THE SAND

1

BROWN BLIZZARD

Dan Willard watched the low-hanging storm clouds roil across the desert like a billowing prairie fire. He dreaded having to drive in the rain. The rubber on the windshield wiper on the passenger side had become so brittle it had split apart and fallen off leaving only the metal part, which when turned on, scratched the hell out of the glass.

Mae had been on him to have a new one put on, but like always, Dan chose to procrastinate, always thinking there was plenty of time.

His neck and back ached from the three-hour drive and there was still another hour before they would reach the Ramada. The first thing he planned on doing once they checked into the motel was to strip out of his sweaty clothes and hop in a cold shower, or if Mae was willing, slip into their bathing suits and jump into the pool to cool down.

Dan heard Mae clear her throat from the front passenger seat. He turned and saw her eyes flick open.

"Where are we?" she asked, stretching out her arms and touching the dashboard with her fingertips.

"Somewhere between here and the middle of nowhere," Dan replied.

"You know what I mean."

"We've got another fifty miles."

Mae let out a loud yawn like a waking lioness. She sat forward in her seat to stare out the windshield. "That looks pretty nasty," she said, referring to the steadily approaching storm front.

"Hope we get there before it starts," Dan replied, praying he was right; vowing to get that damn wiper replaced at the first service station they happened upon.

A bright jag of light shot down from the belly of the dark clouds.

"Did you see that?" Mae said.

A boom of thunder followed a few seconds later and the sun was blocked by the clouds. Even though it was late afternoon, it had suddenly turned dark as if they had just driven into a tunnel.

Dan hit the button on the armrest and lowered his window a couple of inches. He could hear static electricity crackling in the howling wind. Too bad, he was looking forward to that swim in the pool. He put the window back up.

"Sounds like a thunderstorm. Jesus, it better not be a deluge," Dan said. "It rains too hard we could get caught in a flash flood."

"Better not." Mae plucked her harness strap away from her chest so she could lean forward and look out her side of the windshield. "I don't believe it. You never fixed that wiper."

"Hey, I said I would. Next chance we—" but Dan never finished his sentence when a fat raindrop plopped on the glass directly in front of him. Then another raindrop struck the windshield, and then within the blink of an eye, the sky unleashed barrelfuls of metal-pounding rain, the steady barrage ricocheting off the car's hood and roof.

"Oh my God," Mae shouted. "It's really coming down."

Dan switched on the wipers. The rubber blade cleared a crescent path in front of his face while the other wiper on Mae's side scraped the glass annoyingly like Freddie Kruger dragging his gloved knife-like fingers along the basement pipes.

Another bright flash of lightning and Mae let out a surprised yelp.

Dan turned the end of the turn signal lever to increase the speed on the wipers.

It did little to improve his visibility. The road ahead was still a blur, and if that wasn't discouraging enough, he had to deal with the maddening screech of the bare wiper blade repeatedly gouging the windshield.

A loud horn sounded behind them and Dan nearly jumped out of his seat. "What the hell!" He glanced at the review mirror. All he could see was a massive front grill and bumper. "Get off my ass!" Dan screamed.

Mae turned in her seat and looked out the rear window of their RAV4. "Oh my God, Dan, he's going to run us off the road. Pull over, pull over," Mae yelled.

"How? I can't see a thing!" Dan could hear the rumbling of the monstrous diesel engine bearing down on them. It reminded him of the Steven Spielberg movie *Duel* when the oil tanker truck was trying to run the Dennis Weaver character off the road.

The driver behind them sounded his horn again, giving it a couple of sharp blasts.

Dan glanced over his shoulder. "Back off, you son of a bitch!" He turned and gazed out over the top of the steering wheel and couldn't see shit. It was like driving through heavy sprinklers in a carwash. He looked over and saw Mae hunkered down in her seat with her hands clapped over her ears. He had never seen her so scared.

Dan heard the powerful roar of the engine. He looked at his side mirror and saw the front of the big rig in the opposing lane, coming up alongside. He could feel their car being buffeted by the humongous vehicle. He gripped the steering wheel so hard to steady the RAV4 he was afraid he might rip it clear off the column.

As the tractor cab and the trailer in tow passed, the eighteen-wheeler's tires splashed water onto the front of the RAV4 making it impossible for Dan to see.

Dan eased his foot off the accelerator when the big rig's trailer whipped into the lane in front of them. To his relief, the rain let up and seconds later, ceased all together.

"Thank God," Mae said.

Even though the rain had stopped, the dark clouds were still present but they seemed to be moving in a westerly direction away from where Dan and Mae were headed.

Dan watched the rear of the big rig get smaller and smaller as it raced down the road. "Did you get the number off the back of his truck?"

"What number?"

"The one that says 'How's my driving?'"

"No, but I wish I had. He sure was in a damn hurry," Mae said. "I wonder why?"

Dan turned off the wipers. An inverted U-shape was carved permanently in the windshield on Mae's side. Not only was he going to have to replace the stupid wiper blade but now he was going to have to fork out a couple hundred bucks to replace the glass before it cracked from the heat or some trooper pulled them over and gave him a fix-it ticket. He had to admit this vacation was slowly eating away at his wallet.

He glanced in his side mirror to make sure no other big trucks were sneaking up on them and saw a bronze curtain looming behind them. "What is that?"

Mae turned around in her seat to look at the road behind them. "Oh my God, Dan. It that a dust storm?"

It looked like a giant coffee-colored tidal wave and it was moving fast. It had to be almost a mile high and as wide as the eye could see.

"Shit!" Dan said. He thought he might be able to outrun the brown blizzard and stomped on the gas pedal. He watched the needle on the speedometer creep up to 65 then 70. He pushed the speed up to 80. The steering wheel shook in his grip and he could feel the front end of the utility vehicle begin to shimmy, so he reduced his speed back down to 70 but it wasn't fast enough to stay ahead of the swirling storm.

He heard what sounded like light hail hitting the back window then quickly realized it was sandblasting dust striking the car. Dan could see the tiny grains pitting the glass. He could only imagine what the devastating grit was doing to the RAV4's paintjob.

"Dan, stop, get off the road! You can't see a thing!" Mae shouted.

"I would if I knew where 'off the road' was," Dan yelled back. He knew she was right and slowed down. He edged gradually over to where he believed was the shoulder and slowed to a near stop.

The front of the RAV4 took a sudden dip. Dan knew he had screwed up and put the car into a ditch. Thankfully the impact wasn't enough to trigger the airbags.

"Are you okay?" Dan asked.

"Yeah," Mae replied, the fingers of her right hand clutching her shoulder strap.

Dan put the gearshift in reverse and tried to back up but the tires couldn't get traction in the loose sand so he turned off the engine.

The wind howled like a freight train barreling through a tunnel.

"It's no use," Dan said, slamming the top of the steering wheel.

"What are we going to do?" Mae said.

"Guess we'll have to wait it out." Dan unsnapped his seatbelt. He slid forward slightly due to the angle and grabbed the steering wheel to stop himself. The gale shook the car and rattled the side windows. Dan reached up and turned on the dome light. He looked outside and could see sand drifts building up all around the car.

"Oh my God, Dan. What if we're buried alive? Who's going to find us?"

"There's a shovel in the back with our camping stuff. I can always dig us out."

"Not if we suffocate first," Mae said.

"Will you quit with the doom and gloom? We'll be fine."

Mae began to cry.

"Hey," Dan said, and put his hand on her shoulder. "The storm will be over before you know it. Relax. We'll be okay. Of course the car's a total mess," he said with a laugh which put a sheepish grin on Mae's face.

Dan checked his digital wristwatch. It was 8:19. "It should be getting dark by now."

"Please don't tell me we're going to have to stay cooped up in the car all night."

"Once the storm passes, I'll get us out and we can try calling someone."

The sandstorm raged for another twenty minutes.

Everything went dead quiet.

"What now?" Mae asked.

Dan took a moment to assess the situation. The sand had piled up on both sides of the car. There was no telling how deep it was. He didn't want to risk lowering his window and the car filling up with sand.

He glanced over his shoulder and saw a patch of night sky through the rear window. "We can crawl out the back." He pushed the Start button and ran the engine long enough to lower the rear window then shut it down.

A layer of sand maybe six inches thick had poured in, covering some of their gear in the cargo hold.

Dan looked at Mae. "Do you want to go first?"

"Yes. I'm getting claustrophobic. I feel like I'm trapped in a coffin."

"All right," Dan said. "Go ahead."

Mae undid her seatbelt. She turned her body, stretched her leg over the console, and squeezed between the front bucket seats. Kneeling on the rear seat, she pulled herself over and sprawled on top of the sand-covered luggage and camping equipment.

"Careful when you climb out," Dan said. "You don't know what might be out there."

Mae glanced back. "Like what?"

"I don't know. Predators that come out at night."

"Maybe you should go out first."

"Fine. Move over and make room so I can get by you." Dan was struggling to turn around and fit between the bucket seats when Mae screamed.

Something had reached in, grabbed her by the hair, and dragged her out the rear window. Dan had never heard her scream so loud in his life.

"Mae!" Dan lunged across the rear seat. He heard a menacing growl and the sharp clack of teeth snapping together. A sudden wave of fear chilled him to the bone when a spurt of warm blood splashed in his face and Mae stopped screaming.

Before he could call out to his wife, a monstrous beast burst into the car, and with one savage swipe of its razor-sharp claws, slashed open Dan's throat.

2

DESERT VIEW

Ben Lobo put on his short sleeve khaki shirt with the black flaps over the breast pockets. He did up all the buttons except for the top one to reveal the neck of his white tee, and tucked his shirt into his dark brown trousers. He sat in the chair by the foot of the bed and pulled on a pair of black cowboy boots.

He stood and went over to the bureau where he had his gear laid out on the dresser top. After clipping his microphone to his shoulder lapel that was attached to a two-way radio, Ben strapped on the duty belt that also held a pair of heavy duty double lock handcuffs, a dozen tensile strength zip ties, a small canister of police grade pepper spray, a Maglite flashlight, an expandable carbon steel baton, his holstered 10-millimeter Glock 29 and two 10-round capacity magazine clips.

After a quick inspection in the dresser mirror, Ben slipped his green ball cap with the word *Sheriff* in bold yellow letters over his buzz cut and tucked his sunglasses into his breast pocket.

Stepping out of the bedroom, he strolled down the long corridor that was almost blinding from the morning sun shining through the floor-to-ceiling windows that extended around most of the house offering breathtaking views from high atop the bluff looking down at the desert vistas below. Even though it was miles to the nearest neighbor, Ben often felt like he was on display in an aquarium, especially at night when the house was brightly lit up.

He peeked inside Vera's studio, most of the floor covered with paint-splattered canvas tarps, but she wasn't in the room. Her camera equipment was on a table by the window, next to a business office copy machine.

Five easels were set up with partially completed canvases, his wife often working on more than one painting at a time, her process of channeling her creativity, but mostly a way to multitask and speed up production. Eight-by-ten photographs were propped on the trays at the base of four canvases for her to use as her medium source though she preferred going on location and painting real landscapes. A blank canvas was in the corner of the room, no doubt for one of Vera's special projects.

His favorite coffee mug was waiting for him on the Keurig; New Mexico's motto, "Grows as it goes" stenciled on the porcelain along with the red sun symbol of old Spain on a field of yellow. He pushed the blue button and waited for the strong brew to fill up his cup.

Leaving the kitchen, Ben strolled through the open living room with decorative pots of Native American Navajo pottery placed about the perimeter. Handcrafted tapestry rugs covered portions of the mahogany hardwood flooring and maize designs gave the place an authentic ambiance. A round hearth fireplace was situated in the center of the room. On a single wall that ran the width of the house were over twenty of Vera's paintings of picturesque desert landscapes.

Ben strolled past the large sectional couch and matching leather chairs facing the glass panel windows. He opened the sliding glass door, stepped out on the deck cantilevered out from the rocky cliff, and went over to stand by the railing. The morning sun was an orange beacon radiating over the sprawling desert basin below.

He turned and saw his wife sitting on a stool behind a tall easel with a new canvas she was beginning to work on. A small table was beside her with cans of brushes and tubes of various colors of paint. She held an artist palette in one hand and mixed some blue, red, and white together with the tip of her brush, applying them to the canvas in broad strokes for the sky.

"Quite the million dollar view," Vera said.

"You think?" Ben took his sunglasses out of his shirt pocket and slipped them on so as not to burn out his retinas, which made the dawn sky look even more majestic. He glanced over at Vera. In the time he had been standing there, she had nearly completed the top of the canvas. She was nothing short of amazing and would have delighted Bob Ross. Once Ben had watched her complete a 30- by 40-inch canvas of a mountain lake scene in less than twenty minutes.

Vera's artwork was in every major New Mexico gallery throughout the state and she had put on numerous exhibits in New York City. Chances are whenever a person walked into a bank or a business lobby in New Mexico one of Vera's paintings would be hanging on the wall or be displayed on a TV monitor slideshow.

Even though he knew he should be proud of her, it was sometimes difficult knowing that the house they were living in had been bought and paid for, not by Ben's meager salary as sheriff of Yucca Basin, but by what he often referred to in a joking fashion as her 'trifling little hobby.'

"I think I'll take my time with this one," Vera said, though she was almost halfway done.

"Yeah? How much do you plan to get for it?"

"Bernie already has buyers lined up. We can sell this for five thousand easy with my brand," Vera said, speaking of her popularity and her agent that peddled all of her work for a nice fat commission. Personally, Ben thought the guy was a sleaze and was taking advantage of her.

"Sheriff? Are you there?" a female voice crackled on Ben's mike strapped on his shoulder. It was Ben's deputy, Roxy Nez.

Ben reached up and pressed the talk button. "Ben here."

"I have an 11-24 twenty miles out of town on highway 9."

Ben noticed Vera still staring at him. "She found an abandoned car," Ben said, then pushed his talk button. "Go ahead dispatch 11-85," telling Roxy to call for a tow truck.

"You need to come and see this," Roxy said.

"All right." Ben glanced at his watch, and then replied, "ETA thirty minutes."

"Roger, out."

"She's up a little early," Vera said. Even though Vera wouldn't admit it, she was somewhat jealous of Roxy, and rightfully so, as Ben sometimes spent more time with his deputy at the office or out in the field than he did at home with his wife.

Not to mention, Roxy was a smart, attractive young woman with a Navaho heritage and had been crowned prom queen at Yucca Basin High.

Rather than go on to college, Roxy had chosen to sign up at the sheriff's training academy for a rigorous 23-week course in law enforcement and finished in the top ten of her class. Despite her young age and being an inexperienced cadet right out of the academy, Ben recruited her once he learned she was interested in returning home from the apartment she was renting in Albuquerque and serving her community, which she had been currently doing for the past six months.

He had to admit he felt a little protective knowing that it wasn't easy for her moving back home when both her parents had passed while Roxy was a junior in high school and she didn't have any living relatives except for two older brothers that had long moved out—kicked out being a better word—and were constantly in and out of trouble.

Even though Ben thought of Roxy as more of a daughter, he knew Vera didn't share the same sentiment. "I have to go," he said. He went over and kissed Vera on the neck, placing his mug on the edge of her table. "You can finish my coffee if you want. See you later."

Walking toward the sliding glass door, Ben caught Vera's reflection in the glass the exact moment she tossed her paintbrush into his mug.

3

BITS AND PIECES

Roxy had parked the Mustang Police Interceptor well away from the main highway since she had run the vehicle through the self-service carwash earlier that morning as it had been covered in dust from the previous night's sandstorm. The patrol car glistened like a glossy black emerald.

While waiting for Ben to arrive, she had taken the initiative to dig out the sand blocking the front passenger door of the wrecked car that was partially buried in the parabolic dune, using her folding survival shovel she kept in the trunk of her cruiser.

Wearing a pair of disposable blue nitrile gloves, Roxy had gained access to the car and removed the registration card from the glove compartment. The vehicle belonged to Dan Willard, co-owner Mae Willard. By the looks of the camping gear in the back, the married couple had been vacationing in the desert.

Roxy heard an engine approach. A dirty white Chevy Tahoe pulled up and stopped on the shoulder. Ben opened his door with the Yucca Basin Sheriff's Department insignia on the side and climbed out.

A mechanical street sweeper plowed by churning up sand that had deposited on the asphalt. Ben turned his head so as not to be blinded by the swirling grit.

Another large truck followed behind, a vacuum sweeper making the second pass, only this one had sprinklers spurting jets of water intermittently on the cleared road as it went by and left a large puddle of mud by the side of Ben's Tahoe under his door. His truck was dirtier than ever.

"Thanks for nothing," Ben said, scowling at the road maintenance trucks continuing on down the highway.

Roxy looked over at the Mustang cruiser, and smiled. Somehow the flying dust had missed settling on the recently washed patrol car.

Ben trudged along the soft-packed sand over to Roxy.

"Morning."

"Morning, Ben."

"What do you have?"

Roxy handed Ben the registration. "These are the owners."

Ben studied the card. "Came all the way from Yuma." He looked at Roxy. "No sign of them, huh?"

"You better take a look inside," Roxy said.

Even though it was mostly buried in the sand drift, the raised RAV4 chrome emblem was visible on the back door of the utility vehicle. The rear window had been lowered all the way down.

Ben stepped up to the back bumper.

"Before you—"

Upon sticking his head in the opening, Ben immediately backed away and waved his hand in front of his face. "Jesus, you might have warned me."

"I was trying to. Sorry. It's pretty bad."

Roxy watched Ben cover his nose and mouth with his hand and take another look inside the car, his eyes watering from the stench. The headliner and the inside of the windows were speckled with blackish blood splatter. Swarms of black flies congregated on pieces of raw meat that had to be human flesh as there were tattered strips of clothing stuck to the chunks.

"What do you think?" Roxy asked. "Puma?"

"A big cat wouldn't take both of them."

"Coyotes, maybe?"

"I doubt they would be bold enough to jump into the car and drag away the bodies."

"You don't think someone saw they were in trouble and stopped?" Roxy said.

"What, like a Good Samaritan?"

"Or someone else."

"See a chainsaw lying around anywhere?"

Roxy knew he was playing with her even though she could tell by the look in his eyes he took the situation seriously. It wasn't uncommon for people to up and disappear, especially in the desert. "Maybe they wandered off and got lost."

"Let's take a little walk," Ben said. "Better grab your twelve gauge and a trauma bag." While Roxy went back to the cruiser to retrieve her gear, Ben grabbed a canteen and locked up the Tahoe.

Once they were ready, they started out onto the flat playa.

"I doubt we'll find any tracks after that storm, but you never know," Ben said.

Roxy and Ben marched across the sand through the thin vegetation of creosote bushes and bullet-shaped cacti with needle spines. They stayed clear of small piles of rocks that might serve as ideal hiding places for rattlers and coral snakes; one strike of their venomous bites fatal if not treated right away, which was one reason Roxy had brought along the emergency medical kit.

She scanned the ground ahead and spotted something in the sand. "Over there," she said and pointed.

Ben walked over and dropped to one knee. He found a twig that had fallen from a nearby honey mesquite tree and used it to prod the sand.

Roxy stood behind Ben and looked down over his shoulder while he cleared away the sand partially covering a blood-stained left hand. The thumb and forefinger had been chewed off. A woman's wedding band was on the ring finger.

He continued to scoop away the sand unveiling more of the body. "Ah, jeez," he said when he uncovered the mutilated face. "I'm beginning to think that she didn't get lost in the storm, and whatever did this, buried her out here."

"That's something a big cat would do."

"Exactly," Ben said.

"You want me to keep looking for the husband?"

"Go ahead," Ben said, and then glanced up. "Be careful. Whatever did this could still be out here."

Roxy nodded and walked with her tactical shotgun in the ready position, her right hand gripping the stock behind the trigger guard, her left hand on the ratchet if she should suddenly need to ram a shell in the chamber in the event of a large predator attack.

A quick glance at her wristwatch told her that it was only 9:00 AM. She could already feel the desert heat on her face, the fabric of her uniform warming her body, the hot sand baking the soles of her feet through her boots. She'd often laugh whenever she heard Ben complaining about the scorching temperatures, especially when it got in the three-digits.

Roxy's credo was always "The hotter, the better." She was thankful to her Navajo heritage for making her a strong-willed woman though it was her devoted father that taught her how to survive in the harsh desert.

When she turned 14-years-old, her father began driving Roxy to remote regions of the Chihuahua Desert and dropping her off with a full canteen of water, a hunting knife, and only the clothes on her back, expecting her to find her own way home.

She would endure sweltering heat by extracting eatable fruit and drinkable liquid from both the prickly pear and barrel cactus. Able to create her own fire with a self-made hand drill, Roxy feasted on cooked jackrabbit, king snake, and even roasted scorpions.

Often she would have to set up a temporary shelter for the night, the grueling hikes back taking her sometimes two or three days.

She figured if her brothers had survived the same punishment, so could she.

Roxy heard the drone of flies on the other side of a purple flowered Indigo bush just up ahead.

She stepped around the shrub and saw a bloody trail of intestines strung out on the sand next to the man facedown on the ground. His clothes had been ripped to ribbons leaving his viciously slashed back and buttocks exposed. His left arm had been wrenched from the shoulder. She spotted the missing limb lying in a clump of beargrass.

The right leg had been chewed off at the knee leaving a stump of splintered bone.

She looked down and saw a paw print with claw marks on the ends of four widely spaced toes in front of a very large pad. Even though it was huge, she knew it wasn't a mountain lion as big cats rarely left claw marks and these impressions were too elongated. She saw another paw print six feet apart from the other one, which meant it had a very long stride, considering the length of her gait was normally 24 inches.

Whatever it was, it appeared to be walking not on four, but two legs.

Roxy continued to follow the trail, which ended abruptly when the ground hardened on a flat span of bedrock.

She gazed back, and when she was sure Ben couldn't see her, she removed the tracks with the bottom of her boots.

4

THE HEALER

Miguel Walla spotted an official looking white SUV with emergency lights on the roof and a black police cruiser abandoned on the shoulder of the road. He slowed his truck, leaned on the steering wheel, and glanced over at his wife, Maria, who was staring out the passenger window.

"Do you see anyone? I don't," Maria said.

"I want to see." Their 9-year-old daughter, Sophia, stood up in the crew cab, both hands on the top of the front seat.

Maria turned around. "Sophia! Put your seatbelt back on."

"Ah, Mom."

"Better do as she says. The last thing we need is an out-of-state ticket."

They gazed at the vehicles parked suspiciously on the side of the road but didn't see any law enforcement officers around.

"That's odd," Maria said. "Wonder where they went?"

"Who knows?" Miguel said. After they drove by, he sped back up to the posted speed limit.

Miguel glanced over his shoulder. "Seatbelt." He heard Sophia plop back on the seat and waited for the click of the buckle. "Thank you."

"What's it been, five years since the last time we were out here?" Maria said.

"Something like that," Miguel replied. "Hard to believe."

"What did Camilla sound like when you talked to her on the phone and told her we were coming?"

"She's excited to see Sophia."

Maria turned in her seat so she could face Sophia. "Wait till she sees how big you've grown. You were only four last time she saw you."

"I wish we could bring Rosie," Sophia said.

"I know, but it's better she stay with Jack and Nora while we're away. It's much too hot here and Abuela doesn't have air-conditioning."

"Does she still have Astuto?"

"Oh, I'm sure she does," Miguel chimed in.

"When are we going to eat?" Sophia asked.

"Soon." Miguel turned off the main highway and drove onto a dirt road that stretched for miles into the desert. He glanced in the rearview mirror and saw a plume of dust trailing behind them. "We should be at Abuela's in another twenty minutes." Abuela was Sophia's pet name for Camilla; a Mexican nickname many children called their grandmother meaning 'dear grandma.'

Even though the crude road was not a public thoroughfare it was marginally drivable despite enduring years of erosion and wind, and the occasional flash flood—the rest of the way bumpy and jarring.

Finally, Miguel saw Camilla's house nestled at the base of a mesa. The modest home was mission style with a salmon colored tile roof slanted over a large front porch with a white railing and two support posts on either side of the front steps. An armchair, rocker, and porch swing were by the front screen door.

A garden area was on one side of the house along with a chicken coop and a rusty pickup truck twenty years older than Miguel's Ford F-150.

A dust-covered sedan that could have been green or blue was parked ten feet away from the front of the house.

Miguel pulled under the shade of a yucca pinterest that was actually two trees that had grown from one stalk with bare trunks and green pointed leaves at the tops that looked like spiked hairdos. He turned off the engine.

Sophia unbuckled her seatbelt and stood up. "Well, aren't we going in?"

"Not yet," Miguel said.

"Why not?"

"Abuela has company," Maria said, glancing at her cell phone. "Oh darn. Looks like we're not going to get a signal out here."

"I could have told you that. Welcome to the desert." Miguel undid his seatbelt harness and twisted around with his back against the door so he could see his daughter. "Your grandmother helps people in the area."

"You mean she's a doctor?"

"Not exactly. She's what's called a healer."

"Abuela's a shaman," Maria said.

"What's that?"

"It's like a medicine man, or in your grandmother's case, a medicine woman."

"Does she do magic?" Sophia wanted to know.

"Somewhat," Maria said.

The front screen door opened and an elderly man in his eighties stepped out onto the porch. He looked spry for his age and did a little dance before racing down the steps.

"Did he just do a jig?" Maria said.

A woman came out of the house. She wore a tight bandana head wrap and a faded blue denim shirt, a long red, orange, and black tri-colored skirt, and gray cowboy boots.

“That’s Abuela!” Sophia shouted.

Miguel rolled down his window and waved to his mother.

She waved back and called down to the old man. “You forgot these,” she said and held up a pair of crutches.

“I don’t think I’ll be needing them, thanks to you, but I’ll take them just the same.” He ran up the steps and collected his crutches. He went down to his car, opened the driver’s-side door, threw the crutches into the backseat, got in, and sped off like the town crier wanting to spread the news.

“As you can see, Abuela’s quite the miracle worker,” Maria said to Sophia.

The family got out of the truck.

“Come here child and let me see you,” Camilla said with open arms.

Sophia dashed across the yard for a big hug.

“I see you have another satisfied customer,” Miguel said, referring to the man that had just left.

“Amazing what a little peyote gel will do for sciatica.” Camilla looked down at Sophia and smiled. “Now aren’t you the little desert flower?”

“Mom says I’m growing like a weed.”

“Many of my medicinal herbs are weeds,” Camilla said. She looked at Miguel and Maria. “Are you all hungry?”

“Starved,” Miguel replied.

“Come inside.”

Maria and Sophia followed Camilla into the house while Miguel grabbed the luggage from the truck.

Miguel came in through the front room, which was sparsely furnished with a single armchair, a couch, a cluttered coffee table, and no television. He stowed the bags in the spare room, and then joined the others in the kitchen. He could smell freshly baked bread straight out of the outdoor kiln and the tantalizing aroma of different spices.

Sophia was already sitting at the large table that was nothing more than an oak plank with long benches on the sides and a miss-matching chair at each end.

Lunch was an oval platter of smoked chicken and boiled potatoes, a bowl of pinto beans with chopped onions, a basket of oven-baked bread, a dish of agave nectar sweetener, and a large pitcher of sun tea.

“This looks wonderful,” Maria said, placing the last of the cutlery and plates on the table. She sat down on the bench next to Sophia. Miguel occupied the bench directly across from her so he could be next to Camilla at the head of the table.

“So, how was your drive?” Camilla asked, motioning for everyone to start serving themselves.

"Not too bad," Miguel said. He grabbed the basket of bread, broke off a piece, and handed the basket to Camilla.

"We saw two police cars on the side of the road on our way over here," Maria said, placing a slice of chicken on Sophia's plate.

"Were they a white Tahoe and a black cruiser?" Camilla asked.

"Yes, you know them?"

"That would be Sheriff Lobo and his deputy, Roxy. Did they see you?"

"No. They were nowhere around. The cars were just sitting there."

"That's odd," Camilla said.

Miguel looked over at Sophia's plate and saw a little hand reach up from under the table and take her piece of chicken. He did his best to keep a straight face.

Sophia had been looking at Camilla and hadn't noticed. She gazed down at her plate and saw that the food was gone. "Hey, where did my chicken go?"

"Sure you didn't eat it," Miguel said, trying not to laugh.

"No! It was right here."

"Here, have another piece." Miguel lifted another strip of chicken off the platter and put it on Sophia's plate. Sophia went to stab it with her fork but the little hand was back, and again, swiped the chicken.

"Hey!" Sophia ducked her head under the table. "I knew it was *you*!"

Miguel turned and watched the small creature climb up on his bench. Standing only two feet tall, the naked Mexican troll looked like a wrinkly old man with a loincloth of matted fur—the thought it might be pubic hair cringe-worthy—covering its genitals and backside. It looked as though someone had dumped white paint over its greenish coarse skin giving it the blotchy texture of dried salt. Completely bald, it had dark deep-set eyes, a flat sausage nose, and a permanent scowl on its face. Half a dozen tiny spikes protruded from the back of its shoulders. It gobbled up Sophia's chicken and expelled a crude belch.

"Astuto! Back to your hole," Camilla said.

The troll grumbled and wiped his slobbery chin with the back of his hand.

"You heard me," Camilla said, narrowing her eyes.

"*Mea ungy*," Astuto mumbled.

"I'll feed you when we're done. Now scoot."

"*Youa meen*." Astuto jumped down from the bench, scampered across the kitchen, and ducked into a small opening in the wall next to the stove.

Everyone at the table laughed, Sophia being the loudest. She looked at Camilla and asked, "I forgot, why did you name him Astuto?"

"Because he's *sneaky*," Camilla replied with a grin.

5

SPECIAL PICKUP

Vera parked her Jeep Gladiator in front of the US Postal Office, a small building constructed of brown brick and a pitched roof. A blue and white banner with the "sonic" eagle corporate logo stretched over the front entrance facing the parking lot.

A chime sounded as soon as she opened the glass door and stepped inside the lobby. A long glass counter with displays of packaging was in the middle of the room for customers to use as a writing surface and preparing shipments. Next to the postmaster's window was a large cork bulletin board with postal regulations and public messages.

She went over to the wall of PO boxes, inserted her key, and opened the compartment. Inside were a couple of bills and the latest issue of *Artnews* magazine. She flipped through the pages to the article she had been waiting to read that not only raved about her work but also spotlighted one of her landscape paintings. Sharing the same page with six other artists it was a tiny blurb with a thumbprint illustration, certainly not what she had expected.

Vera rolled the magazine into a tube with the bills inside and locked her mailbox.

"Ah, I see you got my email," a voice said.

"Sorry I didn't come over sooner," Vera said, walking up to the postmaster window.

"That's quite all right," Fred Fuller replied. Close to retirement, Fred had been Yucca Basin's postmaster for the last forty years and was a fixture around town. Even though he never went anywhere but his home or the post office, Fred always seemed to be privy to everyone else's business. "How is Ben these days? I don't see him much."

"He's fine. I should have two orders."

"That art supply outfit in Albuquerque must love you." Fred made a habit of checking each sender's name and address on every piece of mail that came into his office.

"Yeah, you might say that. There should be a big box filled with canvases. I might have to borrow your cart."

“Not a problem. I’ll be right back,” Fred said and disappeared into the back room.

Vera placed her mail on the counter and the magazine unfurled flat. She heard the front door chime and turned to see who it was. Kane Nez stood in the doorway. He was a brute of a man, well over six feet tall, with dark scraggly shoulder-length hair and a thin rough beard. He was dressed in his usual attire: black T-shirt, black Wrangler jeans, and a pair of leather-worn boots.

As New Mexico was an Open Carry State, she wasn’t surprised to see the black rubber handgrip of his Colt King Cobra sticking out of the clip-on hip holster on his waist belt.

“Well, fancy meeting you here,” Kane said in his gruff voice.

“Run out of stamps?” Vera said snidely. Even though she had never given the man a reason to think she was interested in him, he thought otherwise. There were times when he would appear out of nowhere, at the grocery store or when she would be filling up at the convenient store gas station. She never mentioned it to Ben, afraid of what he might do if he knew Kane was stalking her.

Kane walked over to the counter and looked down at the front cover of the magazine. “Isn’t that the same rag that blasted you?”

“They have a new editor.”

“That was too bad about that columnist. What was his name?”

“Brad Filcher.”

“What did he call you? Oh, yeah,” Kane raised his hand like he was writing in thin air. “Vera Lobo, The Paint-By-Numbers Landscape Artist.”

“Everyone’s entitled to their opinion.”

“Yeah, well it got him killed, now didn’t it?”

“He got mugged in a parking lot.”

“Outside a bar I hear. Must have gone and pissed somebody else off.”

“What do you want Kane?”

“Nothing,” Kane said and leaned on the counter. He looked Vera up and down like a movie producer appraising a fledgling star. “No law against wanting to share the company of a beautiful woman, is there?”

“That’s where you’re wrong, Kane Nez,” Fred said, opening the leaf at the end of the counter so he could push the cart through with Vera’s packages. “You can’t wear that in here.”

Kane looked down at his holstered gun. “Sure I can.”

“Not in a federal building. I’m going to have to ask you to leave or I’ll be forced to call the sheriff.”

“Go ahead.”

“Kane, just go,” Vera said.

“Fine. We can continue our talk outside.”

"I don't think so," Fred said. "Regulation applies to the parking lot. No guns."

Kane tapped his finger on the counter and gazed at Vera. "Then I'll be seeing you." He turned and strode out the door.

Vera watched him climb into his Dodge Ram. The suspension on the four-wheeler was raised high so the wheel wells could accommodate the over-sized all-terrain tires.

Kane fired up his truck and rumbled out of the parking lot.

"Thank you," Vera said to Fred.

"No problem. That whole Nez family is nothing but trouble."

"What about Roxy? Is she trouble?" Vera asked.

"She's different."

"What do you mean, different?"

"You know what I mean. If you hold the door, I'll push your stuff out for you. Even help you load up."

"Thanks, I appreciate that." Vera held the door open while Fred guided the cart onto the walkway. She went around to the back of her Jeep and opened the tailgate so Fred could load the packages onto the truck bed.

"Well, enjoy the rest of your day," Fred said.

"I will." Vera hesitated for a moment. "What did you mean by Roxy being different?"

"I don't know her that well, but I always got the sense she and the rest of her family never got along. Probably why she moved away."

"So why did she come back?"

"Don't know. Guess because your husband gave her a job."

"Thanks again." Vera gave Fred a wave and got in her truck. She drove out on the main road and headed for home.

6

TAKING A STROLL

Miguel, Maria, and Sophia went behind Camilla's house and walked along the shale stepping stone walkway toward a small compound of animal pens and a stable covered with a corrugated aluminum roof. Camilla stood by two horses in separate stalls, their chins resting on the top of the fence gates.

"This is Poco," Camilla told Sophia and stroked the ear of the gray horse with black leopard spots covering its legs and entire body. "Poco is an Appaloosa."

"He looks like a firehouse dog," Sophia said.

"She means a Dalmatian," Maria said and looked at the other horse. "I love the markings on that one."

Camilla gave the other horse her attention and rubbed under its chin. It had large white patches on its predominately brown hide. "Scout's a pinto. If you like child, tomorrow you can go for a ride."

"Can I?" Sophia said, looking up at her father.

"Sure," Miguel said, giving his consent then glancing over at Maria.

"Only if one of us goes along."

"Hey Poco," Miguel said and walked up to the horse.

"Here, give him this." Camilla reached inside her skirt pocket and took out a hard cookie. She handed it to Miguel.

"What is it?" he asked.

"It's a little concoction I came up with: molasses, curly mesquite, some grama grass. They love it."

Miguel offered the cookie to Poco. The horse snapped its large teeth, nearly taking off Miguel's fingers. "Whoa, maybe he loves it too much."

Camilla, Maria, and Sophia broke out laughing.

"Give him another one, Papa," Sophia said.

"I don't think so," Miguel replied.

"Come child, let me show you the other animals." Camilla took Sophia by the hand and led her over to the individual corrals. Miguel and Maria watched while Camilla showed Sophia a feral donkey named Gus she had found near starvation lying out in the desert while a bunch of hungry vultures waited a few feet away for it to die. Next Camilla let Sophia pet her two pigmy goats, a ram and a milking doe.

When Camilla started to take Sophia over to the chicken coop, Miguel got Camilla's attention and said, "I think Maria and I are going to go for a walk."

"Tread softly," Camilla said.

"We will."

"What did she mean by that?" Maria asked once they were twenty yards from the house.

"That we should watch our step. Even though it doesn't look like it," Miguel glanced about the barren desert of scattered cacti and shrubs, "there's plenty of wildlife out here."

Maria looked around. "Must be hiding because I don't see anything."

"You will."

They had gone maybe a hundred yards when Miguel noticed a pattern in the sand and pointed at the ground. "Know what that is?"

Maria leaned forward with her hands on her knees and studied the long indentation that went along in the sand and was narrower than her little finger. On either side were little choppy markings. "I have no idea."

"Want to find out?"

"Okay."

"Let's see where it leads us." Miguel made sure not to step on the impressions. It took them to a small pile of rocks. Reaching down, Miguel removed a few stones then stepped back. "There's our little tour guide."

"Oh my God. Is that a scorpion?"

"An Arizona bark scorpion to be exact."

"In New Mexico?" Maria said skeptically.

"Go figure."

"Is it dangerous?"

Miguel watched the brown scorpion open its pinchers and curl its stinger over its body. "Enough to make you wish you never got stung."

"I worry about Sophia."

"We'll just have to keep an eye on her, that's all. Let's give this guy back his privacy," Miguel said and put the rocks back.

A minute later, Miguel heard a rattling. He spotted something coiled under a tarbush and immediately grabbed Maria by the arm.

"What is it?" she said, having not heard the sound.

"Stay perfectly still." He motioned toward the small shrub.

"Miguel, that's a rattlesnake."

"A diamondback. Let's keep our distance."

"Maybe we should go back."

"Good idea."

They gave the snake a wide berth and took another way back to Camilla's house.

"Maybe we shouldn't have brought Sophia out here. It's too dangerous."

"Maria, scorpions and rattlers are everywhere. Even where we live."

"It just seems—"

"Hold on," Miguel said, spotting a tight group of hoof tracks in the sand made by a small herd.

"What in the world are those?" Maria asked. "Please don't say wild boar."

"At first I thought they were peccary but they have two-toed hooves. These are different. These have three toes. I've seen this before."

"When?"

"The last time Jack and I were near the border hunting down cryptid specimens for Wilde's zoo."

"My God, Miguel," Maria said. "That was so long ago."

"I know. These tracks are old and they're going away from the house. A migratory pack maybe. I'll mention it when we get back."

"Why, what are they?"

"Chupacabras."

7

QUICK STOP

Ben pulled up to the concrete island outside the Quick Stop convenience store, shut off the engine, and got out of the Tahoe. He grabbed the nozzle off the gas pump and stuck it into the filler tube. After running his credit card through the reader, he leaned back against the rear bumper while the meter noisily clicked off the amount of gallons feeding into his tank.

Having spent more than three hours standing under the scorching sun in ninety-degree heat, Ben was dying for an ice-cold drink.

He spotted three vehicles passing his way on the main road.

Ben raised his hand in a casual wave. Roxy gave him a short blast from her car horn, heading up the small convoy in her Mustang.

A dark blue van—CORONER in bold white letters on the side—was close behind, followed by a flatbed tow truck carrying the Willard's RAV4.

As soon as the pump turned off, Ben replaced the nozzle, and went inside the store. He greeted the clerk standing by the checkout counter. "Hey, Macy."

"Sheriff," Macy Brown replied cordially. A single mom with two kids in high school, Macy knew the struggles of raising a family all on her own. Not that her husband had been a deadbeat. Dalton Brown had been a decent hardworking man and loving father. He'd been a pillar to the community and was always willing to help out a stranger. Which was why he ended up dead after picking up a hitchhiker—an escaped convict on the run—and was left on the side of the road and Macy pregnant with their second child.

"I guess you saw it on the news. He hit another one of your stores upstate," Ben said, referring to a string of gas station robberies.

"So, is it true? That he killed the clerk with a hunting knife?" Macy asked.

"I'm afraid so. He's no longer just a robber. Headlines are now calling him the Quick Stop Killer."

"My God."

"You have my number on your phone, right?"

"I do," Macy replied.

"Good. First sign of trouble, you call me."

"I will."

Ben strolled down the aisle to the refrigerator units in the back. He grabbed a frosty bottle of vanilla root beer off the shelf, and on his way back to the checkout counter, a large bag of barbeque potato chips and packet of beef jerky.

He knew Vera would have a conniption if she knew. She always scolded him for his poor diet choices. Hey, what she didn't know wouldn't hurt her.

He was setting his items on the counter when the front door opened and in walked Ethan Nez, Roxy's brother. Ethan and her other brother, Kane, shared an apartment together in a rundown tenement on the outskirts of town, a lowlife hangout for deadbeats and druggies. Ben should know, he spent more hours than he cared to count patrolling the area, settling family disturbances, and breaking up fistfights.

"Hi, Macy, how are you?" Ethan said.

"Doing fine, Ethan. How about yourself?"

Ben listened to the two bantering back and forth like a couple of infatuated teenagers as though he wasn't in the room. He'd heard rumors that Ethan was keen on Macy and that they had gone out a few times, mostly to the Mesa Bar just out of town.

Even though Ben held a high regard for Macy, he knew she wouldn't have much of a future dating someone like Ethan Nez, who he thought was a lost cause and would never amount to much. He figured for Macy, it was a way to pass the time.

Once, Ben had voiced his concern to Roxy about her brothers but she let him know right up front that she did not want to have that discussion. Ben knew she favored Ethan over Kane. He also knew she shared something in common with Ethan. They both feared Kane, and rightfully so, as Kane was one mean son-of-a-bitch. Just ask the guys whose jaws he broke or the ones that got stomped half to death. When it came to receiving a beating from Kane, it was always best to keep your mouth shut.

"So Sheriff, how's my baby sister doing?" Ethan said.

"What do you mean?"

"Is she cutting the mustard?"

Ben looked at Ethan.

The man had a grin on his face with a hint of defiance, a trait he picked up from Kane—the intimidating look of a bully.

"You mean, is she a good officer? Yeah. I think she has a great career ahead of her. Why, does that have you worried?"

Ethan immediately lost the attitude. "Just asking."

Ben gave Macy a twenty and she gave him his change. "If you'll excuse me, I have to head over to the morgue."

"Why's that, Sheriff?" Macy asked. "Someone die?"

"Can't really talk about it. All I can tell you is we found two bodies out in the desert."

"What, did they get caught in the storm?" Ethan asked.

"No, they were attacked."

"Attacked?" Macy said. It wasn't often something newsworthy happened in Yucca Basin.

"What, like an animal attack?" Ethan said.

Ben studied Ethan's face. "What makes you think that?"

"I don't know. You said 'attacked' and I thought some animal killed them."

"Well, we won't know until after the autopsy." Ben raised his drink and bags of goodies. "Be seeing you."

"Bye, Sheriff," Macy said.

8

ROUTINE STOP

Kane wanted nothing better than to go back and beat the holy shit out of that little shit, Fuller. Maybe one day he would pay the postmaster a visit and do just that. He was so pissed he hadn't realized his speed until he heard the siren. He glanced in his rearview mirror and saw Sheriff Lobo's Tahoe following close behind with the roof rack lights flashing.

"Shit!" Kane wondered if the sheriff had seen him inside the post office trying to pick up on the man's wife. It was bad enough the sheriff had a personal vendetta cruising by the apartments looking to nab someone dealing drugs, now Kane had to worry the man was going to hound him knowing Kane was interested in his wife.

He tried to think if there was anything in his truck that could land him in jail. He wasn't sure, but he didn't think so.

He reduced his speed and pulled over to the shoulder of the road. He shut off the engine, lowered the driver's window, and put both hands on the steering wheel. Kane glanced at his side mirror. The sheriff was taking his sweet time getting out of his vehicle. Most likely he was running Kane's license plate on his computer while the dash cam recorded the traffic stop.

Sheriff Lobo climbed out of his Tahoe. He walked alongside Kane's Dodge Ram truck and stopped short of the driver's window, one hand on the butt of his service weapon.

Kane kept his hands on the steering wheel. He turned his head to look up at the sheriff and said, "You know I'm a valid CCW holder," meaning that he had a permit to carry a concealed weapon and by fully disclosing there was a firearm in the vehicle he hoped to avoid any misunderstanding that could result in an altercation.

"Where?"

"On my right hip."

"Do me a favor and keep your hands where I can see them."

"Sure thing," Kane said.

"Do you know how fast you were going?"

"Uh, no, not really."

"Yeah, well, that's not why I pulled you over."

Kane looked at the sheriff but he couldn't read his expression as the man was wearing sunglasses. "Then why did you pull me over?"

The sheriff leaned in. "Let's just say, I'm on to you."

"I don't know what you're talking about."

"Sure you do."

Kane flexed his fingers but knew it would be a big mistake to remove his hands from the steering wheel.

"Sooner or later, you're going to slip up. That goes for your brother too. And when you do, I'll be waiting."

"Someone might call this harassment."

"Consider it a warning."

So this didn't have anything to do with Lobo's wife. In a way, Kane was relieved even though he knew they would have to be extra careful dealing drugs out of the apartment complex.

"I'd obey the speed limit if I were you," Sheriff Lobo said. He slapped the side of the door. "You have a good day."

Kane watched the sheriff turn his back and walk to his vehicle. Kane's right hand dropped onto the handgrip of his revolver strapped to his side. He glanced around at the desolate terrain, not a single car on the highway.

It would be so easy.

9

RED DEVILS

Sophia was surprised the walk-in chicken coop was so big. She counted at least fifteen chickens free grazing for feed strewn about the sand inside the large area protected by heavy-duty mesh wire fencing that also included the overhead to prevent varmints from climbing inside. The plywood wall interior was roomy, about half the size of her bedroom at home. One wall comprised of twenty nesting beds, five across and four rows high of which six broody hens were nestled over their boxes.

"This is a good time to collect some eggs while most of them are out in the yard," Camilla said and handed Sophia a small basket. "Don't disturb the chickens sitting on their eggs."

"Why? Won't they just move?"

"Chickens can get a little cranky, especially when they think you're stealing their eggs. It's a hormonal thing."

"What's that?" Sophia asked.

"Something you'll learn about when you're older. Trust me. Go ahead and get me about a dozen so I can do some baking."

Sophia started at one end and made her way across the bottom row of nesting boxes that were unoccupied. When she discovered her first egg, she grabbed it and held it up for her grandmother to see.

"Very nice."

Before Sophia put the egg in the basket, she inspected it. The otherwise white shell had a few places that were covered with a black crust. "There's something on it."

"It's just a little poop."

"Ew, yuck. There's never poop on our eggs."

"That's because you buy them from the store. You don't think there's someone that cleans them first?"

"I never thought about it."

"Don't worry. It comes right off. Besides, who eats the shell?"

Sophia continued gathering eggs. She made the mistake of getting too close to one of the broody hens and almost got pecked on the hand. "Stop that!" Sophia said, scolding the ornery bird, and then moving along.

With her basket nearly filled, Sophia was reaching for an egg in a nesting box on the top row when it suddenly disappeared in the straw covering the bottom. "Hey!"

"What's wrong?" Camilla asked.

"The egg. It was right here. Now it's gone."

Camilla put her hands on her hips and shouted, "Astuto! Put that back!"

Sophia rose up on her tiptoes so she could see the back of the box and used her hand to clear away the straw. She saw a chewed away hole the size of an orange and Astuto's face staring back at her. "I see him!"

"You're in big trouble mister," Camilla said and stormed out of the hen house.

Sophia began to rush out after her, but when she realized she was carrying a batch of fragile eggs, she slowed down so as not to break them. When she came out and walked around the side of the coop, her grandmother was nowhere to be seen. Figuring she might have doubled back to the stable, Sophia went another way and found herself in what at first appeared to be a vacant pen, and then she saw the Mexican troll.

He was standing in a small mound of overturned dirt. His two-foot tall body was completely covered in tiny red insects from head to toe.

Sophia dropped the basket. She ran over and saw red ants swarming over Astuto though he didn't seem to mind. Her immediate reaction was to slap them off. She bent down and started brushing them off Astuto's chest and arms. Each time she removed the ants off of the troll, some of them would cling to her hands and crawl up her arms, creating tiny pinpricks of pain. Soon it became so intense she screamed.

"What is it, child?" Camilla said, suddenly appearing. As soon as she saw the ants on Sophia, her grandmother used her bare hands and swiped them off but by then Sophia had been bitten numerous times.

Sophia's parents raced into the pen.

"What's happened?" her father shouted.

Camilla turned. "Fire ants. Miguel, take Sophia into the house."

Sophia's father rushed over and gathered her up in his arms.

"What about Astuto?" Sophia said. "Who's going to help him?"

"They can't hurt him," her grandmother assured her. "His skin is so tough he can't feel a thing."

Everyone rushed into the house. Sophia was crying by then as her father sat her down on a bench at the table.

Camilla opened a kitchen cabinet and took out a tube of ointment. She began dabbing the cream on every welt. "This should stop the blistering. Don't worry, the salve should take the pain away."

It took Sophia a couple of minutes before she stopped crying. "It doesn't hurt anymore."

"Thank God," Sophia's mother said and gave her a hug.

Sophia heard tiny footsteps at the backdoor and saw Astuto standing in the threshold, still covered in ants.

"You better not bring them in here," Camilla said. She went over and cleaned the ants off the troll, each time rubbing her palms together and grinding them up.

Sophia could see them crawling all over her grandmother's arms. They had to be eating her alive. It took maybe a minute or two for her grandmother to rid the troll of the insects and to smash the ones creeping on her.

Once all the ants were dead, her grandmother shooed Astuto out the door.

"Abuela, are you okay?" Sophia asked.

"Yes, child, I'm fine."

"Aren't you going to use the ointment?" Sophia looked at her grandmother's hands and arms and saw not a single bite mark.

10

PRELIMINARY EXAM

Ben sat in the Tahoe behind the Coroner's Office and ate the last of the chips and then crumpled up the bag. He pulled an antibacterial wipe out of the pouch in the cup holder and cleaned his hands before getting out of the truck. Instead of going around to the front, Ben chose to enter the building through the rear service door next to the dumpster.

Once inside, he walked down a short hallway that led to a small office area with two desks, some filing cabinets, and a table with a copy machine, coffee maker, and an open package of reamed paper. Off to the right was a door with the single word MORGUE stenciled on an opaque glass window.

Ben opened the door and stepped inside the examination room flooded with bright overhead fluorescent lights. It was glaring enough to make him almost want to put on his sunglasses tucked in his breast pocket. The room was about as big as a walk-in freezer in a supermarket and was just as frigid. Four stainless steel doors occupied one wall: storage lockers for human bodies. A table was tucked in the corner with a scale; the type butchers used to weigh lunchmeat.

Everything cold and stark, a metal desk and a plastic chair, human anatomy illustrations tacked on a corkboard, notes scribbled on a marred white board.

The naked corpses of Dan and Mae Willard were on the two autopsy tables situated in the center of the room. Long pipes designed to funnel bodily fluids elbowed down from the underside of the tables to the drain on the sloped floor. A gurney with the two black cadaver bags used for the deceased was parked against the wall next to a stainless steel commercial sink.

Even though he had watched the man and woman be exhumed from the sand and placed in body bags, Ben hadn't realized the true extent of their injuries. Seeing the bodies fully exposed under the bright light and the skin rinsed off, Ben was so appalled by the carnage that he had to look away for a moment and put his hand over his mouth when the contents in his stomach went for an acid reflex ride into his mouth.

"If you have to do that, please step outside," a voice said.

Ben turned and saw Keith Monroe. The coroner was a short, balding man in his mid-fifties and must have been returning from having a smoke outside as he was slipping his disposable lighter inside a hard pack of cigarettes in the front pocket of his white lab coat.

Not able to speak, Ben rushed over to the sink. He turned the handle on the spigot, spat into the sink, and ducked his head under the faucet to take a drink.

"Never thought of you as being the squeamish type."

"Must have been something I ate," Ben replied, shutting off the water. He turned around and noticed a white five-gallon plastic pail under Dan Willard's examination table, containing the man's severed left arm and a clear plastic bag filled with a grisly slop of internal organs collected from the crime scene.

As each victim had been attacked differently, the husband had been placed facedown as most of his lacerations were on his back whereas the wife was lying face up.

At first, Ben thought Monroe had already performed the brain autopsy on the woman where he would have to make an incision and pull the scalp down over her face before using a cranium saw to remove the cap of the skull. But then he noticed a bit of white on the top of her head and realized what he was seeing was the savagely mauled tissue of what had once been her face.

"Any idea how long they'd been out there?" Ben asked.

"Not long," Monroe said. "Whatever blood they had left in their bodies has collected in their lower extremities causing livor mortis."

"The purplish coloring around the midsections and legs."

"That's right. They were killed within the last twenty-four hours. I'll be able to narrow it down after I do a proper autopsy."

Ben stepped over and gazed down at the husband. He studied the stump where the right leg should have been. He was surprised to see that the kneecap was still attached, the shinbone being gnawed away just below that. He turned his attention to the deep gashes on the man's back. "Any idea what kind of animal could have done this?"

"Well, I've seen plenty of animal attack victims and the extensive damage that claws can do. Big cats can get as long as two inches. Grizzlies have claws that can grow up to four inches long. They can tear through a person's flesh like a meat cleaver right down to the bone." Monroe reached inside his coat pocket and took out a depth gauge similar to what a mechanic might use to measure the tread depth of a tire, only lengthier. He inserted the end into the deepest cut. He removed the instrument and checked the marking. "Holy crap."

"How deep is it?"

The coroner gave Ben a concerned look. "Nearly six inches."

"That's impossible. There's nothing around here with claws like that."

"There is now."

"So what you're telling me is there's an apex predator out there somewhere with claws longer than a grizzly?" Ben said.

"That's right, Sheriff."

PART TWO

CAMILLA'S TALE

11

THE STORYTELLER

Camilla had Miguel, Maria, and Sophia join her out on the porch where she had a large pitcher of sun tea brewing by the front steps. Miguel and Maria sat on the swing seat, while Sophia sat in the rocker next to Camilla who made herself comfortable on the large chair covered with cowhide and a cushioned back. Astuto was off somewhere, most likely getting into some kind of trouble.

"Maria, would you like to set us up with drinks before I begin?" Camilla said.

"Sure." Maria got up and grabbed the glass pitcher by the handle. Four tall glasses filled with ice were on a small table to the right of the screen door. She poured the sun-brewed tea and gave everyone a glass, and then sat back beside Miguel who was swaying gently in the porch swing.

Camilla took a moment to sip her drink. She placed the glass down on the deck beside her chair where it would be out of the direct sun, which was an hour away from setting. She looked at Sophia and smiled. "I have never told you this story."

"Which story is that?" Sophia asked, eagerly waiting.

"About your great-great grandmother. Her name was Lizzy." Camilla shot a glance over at Miguel. He grinned and gave her a nod, having heard the tale before. She knew it was one of his favorites.

"No, I have never heard it before," Sophia said, holding her glass on her lap with both hands.

"Back in those days," Camilla began, "the territory here was often called The Fiendish Badlands, and for good reason."

"And why was that?" Sophia asked.

"It was very bad back then."

"You mean outlaws?"

"Oh, there were those. No, I'm talking about things much worse. Things you wouldn't think could be real but are. Do you have an open mind, Sophia?"

Sophia looked to her mother for the answer.

"Remember we always say never to prejudge anything until you know for sure if it's true or not," Maria said.

"Yes," Sophia answered right away. "Is that keeping an open mind?"

"It sure is," Miguel piped in, anxious for his daughter to hear the story. He smiled at his mother. "I think Sophia's ready."

"Well," Camilla said, "it all began..."

12

THE NAGUALS

The saddle creaked as the bounty hunter leaned on the pommel and surveyed the ruination of the homestead. A few charred timbers were still aglow, collapsed in front of the stone chimney. Posts from the split rail fencing had been heaved from the ground and the Guernsey and the plow horse that had resided within the extirpated corral had been maliciously mutilated and sundered. The marauders had even trampled the flowerbed and the small vegetable garden.

The buckskin champed on the bit and stamped a hoof on the hard clay.

"Easy, boy," the bounty hunter said, his face shadowed under the six-inch brim of the weathered Stetson; the stampede string hanging down, touching the war rag bundled around his neck. He weaved his glove through the long shock of black mane in front of him and gently stroked the muscular shoulder to soothe the skittish horse.

Holding onto the pommel with one hand, he swung his leg over the cantle and dismounted.

Trail dust shook from his long coat as he stepped back and turned, one hand pulling back the front of his slicker to reveal the holstered .44-caliber Colt Dragoon. The dying man who the bounty hunter had appropriated the gun from had bragged it was the same revolver once owned by James Butler, otherwise known as Wild Bill.

The bounty hunter reached up, and from behind his bedroll, pulled out his Ithaca 10-gauge shotgun he had used on his short stint as a young man riding guard for the Butterfield Overland Stage. He flipped open the twin 12-inch long barrels, checked them for full loads, and snapped the coach gun shut.

The jingle bobs on the rowels of his spurs clinked as he strode over to where the bladed head of a long heaved ax was buried into a stump, next to a severed arm still wearing a tattered shirtsleeve.

The bounty hunter stepped around the stump. He saw more butchered body parts and reckoned it was the farmer, especially when he saw the man's decapitated head upright in the dirt, facing him, looking as though he had been buried in the ground from below the neck down. Even though the face was smudged with blood and grime it was clear to see that he had been a handsome man with tanned youthful features and long brown hair.

And when the head opened his eyes, the bounty hunter saw that they were blue.

"You best not hurt them," the head said.

"And who might you be referring?" the bounty hunter asked, not the least bit alarmed that he was conversing with someone that should rightfully be dead.

"My wife and little girl."

The bounty hunter glanced over at the burnt rubble of the farmhouse. "I'm to assume they did not perish in the fire?"

"No! You took them. Wait a gall darn minute," the head said, and squinted his eyes against the glaring afternoon sun. "You're not one of them."

"No, I'm not," the bounty hunter said. He reached under his long coat and pulled out a folded parchment. He tucked his sawed-off shotgun under his arm, opened up the wanted poster, and showed it to the head. "Is this one of them?"

"That's him! He's their leader."

"How many were there?"

"Five. Scary Injuns they were."

"That they are. Scary. But they're not Injuns."

"Then what in hell's name are they?"

"They're Naguals."

"Never heard of that tribe."

"That's because they're not Injuns."

"Then what are they?"

"Evil incarnations conjured by some diablerie curse."

"You mean like demons?" asked the head.

"Skin-walkers."

"Sounds to me like you've been drinking too much tarantula juice."

"That so? I suggest you look around," the bounty hunter said.

The head glanced to the left then to the right, staring at the dismembered human limbs and the heaps of horrific sanguineous bowels before furrowing his brow and asking, "Who is that?"

"That, my sodbuster friend, is you. Or what is left of you."

"Yeah, then why aren't I dead?"

"Oh, I think you're as good as dead."

"The hell you say."

"One of them put a curse on you. It's medicine man magic. Anyway, I best get going."

"You can't just leave me for the buzzards!"

"Sorry but there's a bounty on this bunch and I need to get after them while their tracks are still fresh."

"But I could help you nab those renegade outlaws."

"How, by jabbering them to death?" the bounty hunter snickered before turning and striding over to his horse.

He tucked the shotgun back behind the bedroll, climbed onto the saddle, and grabbed the reins.

"Please, mister. They...took my family," the head said with a quavering voice as tears rolled down both cheeks.

* * *

The bounty hunter stood up in the stirrups, peered down, and appraised the town below. He panned the shabby rooftops—figuring them for a saloon, livery, general store, hotel, and a couple of other dilapidated structures—before easing back down in the saddle. A dust devil as tall as a hitching post twirled down the main street of the ghost town past the five horses tied up in front of the saloon.

Before the buckskin had carried the bounty hunter up the steep grade onto the ridge of the bluff, they'd passed a perched turkey vulture urinating on a sign riddled with bullet holes and the town's name Hangman's Gulch branded on the plank.

"Looks to me we found them," said the head.

After the bounty hunter had taken pity on the head, he had braided a pigging string in with the head's long strands of hair and then cut a short length of lariat with his 12-inch bowie knife—the hefty blade having been forged out of Damascus steel in Arkansas by the blacksmith James Black—wrapping the rope around the head's forehead for a carrying handle and looped it around the horn.

"What now?" the head asked. "Ride in, guns blazing?"

"What and end up like you?" the bounty hunter replied.

"So how long have you been chasing these skin-walkers?"

"Across seven territories. I have to say, they're a slippery bunch."

"Must be a mighty big reward."

"There's not enough gold in all of Fort Knox to pay for what they've done."

"They must be some cold-blooded heathens," the head said.

"That they'd be."

The head closed his eyes for a moment, then reopened them and said, "Any chance my wife and little girl could still be alive?"

The bounty hunter reached down, grabbed the end of the headband rope and held the head up so that they were facing each other.

"I have to be honest. I'd be betting against it," the bounty hunter said.

"I was afraid you might say that."

"There're two things you should know before we ride down," the bounty hunter said.

"What's that?"

"The Naguals are not what they appear and will show no mercy."

"All right, and what's the other thing?" asked the head.

"Remember that poster I showed you?"

"Yeah."

"Says those Naguals are 'wanted dead, not alive.'"

"That's fine by me."

"You don't understand. Once we kill the Nagual that put the curse on you, you die too."

"Damn if that ain't just my miserable luck."

* * *

Standing a few feet away from the batwing doors leading into the saloon, the bounty hunter took a moment and opened his long coat, giving the head an appraisal of the hardware he was packing.

"Good Lord, you're a one-man regiment," the head said and let out a low whistle as he gazed up, dangling from the bounty hunter's gun belt.

"In my business you have to be." Besides the Dragoon and the bowie knife, the bounty hunter was also armed with a Colt Navy .36-caliber revolver; a two barrel derringer he had confiscated from a cheating card dealer; a throwing tomahawk he had won after a fight to the death with a Navajo warrior; a bayonet he had pulled out of the chest of a Confederate soldier in New Mexico at the battle of Glorieta Pass; a bandoleer of cartridges, and a split hide bullwhip. The coach gun was hidden in the deep pocket of his long coat.

Four leopard-spotted Appaloosas and a white paint with a black head were hitched to the rail, the stallions' chests lathered with white brine from being ridden hard.

The weary horses watched the bounty hunter with mild interest as he walked up to the batwing doors, pushed them open, and stomped into the saloon.

* * *

Three of them were congregated around a table studying the cards in their hands as they intently played a game of Navajo Tens. They wore cloth headbands and long bead strands draped down their chests, over light-colored long sleeve cotton shirts with the shirttails out. Their pants were tucked inside knee-high leather boots. Three Winchester carbines leaned against the table. Not one of the Naguals bothered to glance up as the bounty hunter sauntered by.

A beak-nosed Nagual wearing a top hat and smoking a stogy stood behind the bar.

The bounty hunter unhooked the head from his gun belt and placed him on the bar top.

"Name your poison," stated the beak-nosed Nagual.

"Two whiskeys," the bounty hunter said. "One for me and one for my friend here."

The beak-nosed Nagual slammed two shot glasses on the bar. He grabbed a bottle and pulled the cork out with his rotted teeth and spat the stopper onto the floor. Tipping the bottle, he overflowed the whiskey into each shot glass so that the rotgut ran down the sides. The Nagual sneered and banged the bottle down.

"Can I get a little help here?" the head asked.

The bounty hunter picked up a shot glass, put the rim up to the head's lips and tilted. In one gulp, the head swallowed and the whiskey was gone.

The head shriveled up his face and gasped, "Could use a little more turpentine and cayenne." The whiskey drained down his throat right away, seeped out from the bottom of his stubby neck and formed a circular puddle on the bar.

Downing his whiskey, the bounty hunter casually glanced about the saloon, searching for the fifth renegade outlaw, the honcho Nagual. The only other occupants in the room were three mummified corpses propped up in cheap pine caskets leaning against a wall. They were dressed in dusty black burial suits with the cuffs sewn to the lapels so that their arms were crossed over their chests.

The younger-looking Nagual at the table snatched a card from the discarded pile and tucked it in his hand.

"That's my card!" yelled the burly Nagual.

"You put it down!"

"Be still, or I'll shoot the both of you," the gray-haired Nagual growled, slamming a heavy .45-caliber Colt on the table.

Watching from across the room, the head on the bar glanced up at the bounty hunter and commented, "If we're lucky, these boys might do us a favor and do themselves in."

The two Naguals bolted up from the table, tipping over their chairs, ready to brawl.

"See, what did I tell you," the head said with a smirk.

A door opened behind the bar and out stepped the honcho Nagual. He wore a striped cotton shirt with leather cuffs covering his forearms and short chaps tucked inside his shin-high moccasins. A pair of pearl handle revolvers hung low on his hips. He held a young child and led a woman out by a short tether wrapped around her throat.

"Lizzie, Lizzie, thank God!" shouted the head.

The little girl's eyes brightened at the sound of her father's voice. "Daddy, where are you, Daddy?"

"I'm right here!" the head replied from the bar top.

Lizzie screamed when she saw her father.

The three Naguals at the card table turned and faced the bounty hunter.

The honcho Nagual stepped out from behind the bar with his two captives. "You should have given up long ago, bounty hunter. But as you are here, perhaps you would like to feast with us," he said and yanked the tether so that the woman's slender neck was up to his lips just as his human face transformed into a snarling puma. He buried his sharp fangs deep into her flesh then drew away and reverted back into the honcho Nagual.

"Lizzie!" the head screamed.

The burly Nagual roared as his face jutted into a snout. Keen claws shot out of his stubby fingers. His massive shoulders were bulging out of the split seams of his shirt as he shape-shifted into a black bear. The bounty hunter pulled out the Ithaca shotgun from the long coat and fired both barrels, blowing a hole through the Nagual's chest with silver ball bearings smelted by a superstitious miner living in a cave up on Hermit's Peak.

The saloon shook as the 400-pound bear crashed to the floorboards.

The bounty hunter immediately uncoiled the split hide bullwhip, strung it out with a rapid toss and cast the lash out with a loud snap. A pure silver three-foot section of barbwire attached at the end wrapped around the younger Nagual's neck as he reached for his carbine. The bull-whacker yanked on the taut whip, tearing the Nagual's head clear off his shoulders.

The gray-haired Nagual grabbed his hog-leg off the table, aimed straight for the bounty hunter and fanned the hammer.

Slugs ripped through the bounty hunter's long coat as he returned fire with the Navy Colt and the long-barreled Dragoon.

The exchanged hail of bullets filled the room with smoke.

The gray-haired Nagual threw down his gun and instantly transformed into a giant timber wolf before leaping at the bounty hunter.

And when it pounced, the bounty hunter drove the long silver shank of the bayonet deep into the creature's chest.

The Nagual howled and reared back, clutching the bayonet as it fell dead on the floor.

"You are a brave warrior," remarked the honcho Nagual, releasing the unconscious woman. Blood trickled down her neck as she slumped to the floor.

"Let me go!" Lizzie yelled, kicking her tiny feet.

"Take the brat!"

The beak-nosed Nagual reached over the bar counter and snatched the squirming child from the honcho Nagual.

"Don't you hurt her none!" the head warned.

"Put a bullet in that thing," said the honcho Nagual, his hands hovering over the pistol grips in a gunslinger stance as he faced the bounty hunter for a showdown.

"You don't hurt my Daddy," Lizzie yelled and scratched the beak-nosed Nagual's face before he could reach for his gun.

The bounty hunter flipped open the front of his long coat and pulled out the tomahawk. His shirt was blotched red from his bullet wounds; blood had dripped down his pant legs onto his boots.

"You bring that to a gunfight?" laughed the honcho Nagual. He gripped both gun handles and drew the pistols, cocked back the hammers, and pointed both barrels.

All the while the tomahawk was spinning blade over handle as the bounty hunter had already flung it, its travels ending when it thudded in the honcho Nagual's forehead.

"I finally tracked down the Navajo shaman that changed you into skin-walkers," the bounty hunter said. "I made him lift the curse by blessing that tomahawk before I sent him off to his happy hunting grounds."

The honcho Nagual dropped his guns and reached up to pull the tomahawk out of his skull but the blade was wedged tight, so he kept yanking until it finally came out.

Suddenly a deafening shrill emanated out of the fissure in the honcho Nagual's forehead, and like a tornado swirling down a mineshaft, the honcho Nagual was sucked up inside the hole and vanished.

"Nice trick," said the beak-nosed Nagual before shooting the bounty hunter in the back.

The bounty hunter fell but managed to get off two wild shots from his derringer before hitting the floor.

"You bastard!" the head yelled.

"Oh wait. I forgot to kill you," the beak-nosed Nagual said and aimed his revolver squarely at the head.

"Leave my daddy alone!" Lizzie screamed.

"Shut up, before I rip out your tongue." The beak-nosed Nagual gripped Lizzie behind the neck and pushed her face down on the bar. "Say bye-bye papa."

"Hold on a minute!" pleaded the head. "Aren't you supposed to give a dying man a last request?"

"You want me to save you a slice after I throw her on the spit?"

"Just a last smoke and a whiskey, that's all I ask."

"Sure, why not." The beak-nosed Nagual held onto Lizzie and put his gun down on the bar. He grabbed the whiskey bottle, pouring some into a shot glass. He wrapped his newly forming talons around the glass and held it for the head to drink.

"After the drink, give me my smoke." The head opened his mouth and gulped the entire shot glass.

The beak-nosed Nagual—his face now sprouting tiny feathers—took the stogy out of his mouth and shoved the smoldering cigar into the head's mouth then lit a stick match.

The head waited for the appropriate moment as the flame approached the end of the stogy then spewed out the mouthful of combustible alcohol, catching the Nagual's face on fire. The Nagual released Lizzie and spun around as the flames quickly spread and engulfed his body, the heat from the flames strangely contained. The conflagration raged and within seconds, the Nagual was reduced to a small pile of skeletal ashes.

Lizzie sat up on the bar. "Daddy, we're safe. The bad men are dead."

The head gave his daughter a loving smile, rolled back his eyes, and then, unceremoniously died.

* * *

The woman gazed down at the bounty hunter as he slowly opened his eyes.

They were in one of the hotel's abandoned rooms. The bounty hunter was flat on his back under a blanket, she in a chair beside his bed.

"I dug enough lead out of you to sink a canoe," she said.

"I reckon I owe you."

"Just rest."

"You know, I never did get your name."

"It's Selma."

"And your husband's?"

"Jonathan."

"How's your little girl?"

"She's asleep in the next room."

"If you care to know, my name's Grainger. You should be proud to know that your husband was a good man."

"I know. Now you must rest," Selma said.

She watched over the bounty hunter as he drifted off to sleep, dreading tomorrow as the Nagual's blood coursed through her veins.

13

THE DALTRYS

Grainger drew the horse blanket around his shoulders and stared out the second-story hotel window, watching Selma trudge out of the saloon. She was lugging a severed leg in one hand, the tomahawk in the other. She approached the bonfire burning in the middle of the ghost town's main street and tossed the limb into the flames.

He repositioned his stance, wincing as his wounds flared up.

The bounty hunter heard footsteps approaching down the hall and spun around, lifting his cocked Colt .44-caliber Dragoon out from under the blanket. He pointed at the intruder, and when he realized who it was, quickly raised the barrel and reset the hammer on the firearm.

"Not wise to sneak up on a person," he admonished Lizzie who was standing in the doorway to his room.

"Sorry," Lizzie replied but showed no fear.

"Mind if I get my britches?"

Lizzie snickered and faced away.

Grainger dropped the blanket, snatched his denim trousers off the back of the wooden chair, and sat down on the edge of the swayback bed. Stifling a groan, he slowly slipped his pants over his bandaged legs. He put on his indigo shirt, leaving the front unbuttoned so as not to aggravate the dressings on his chest as he stood.

"You can turn around," he said.

"Momma says you should be dead." It was a direct statement made without malice by a brave little girl that had recently witnessed her father die.

Grainger glanced down at Selma's weeping patchwork on his torso. "Guess I'm lucky to be resurrected."

Lizzie stepped over to the small table by the bed to admire some of Grainger's belongings. She appraised the ornate pocket watch with the antlered stag etched on the silver case and fiddled with the cartridges next to his .36-caliber Navy Colt. She picked up a couple of half-dollar coins and tested their weight in her palm then placed them back on the table.

But it was the penny knife that truly struck her fancy.

Grainger picked up the purposeful tool and demonstrated how the folding blade bent so it could fit inside the wooden handle.

"Makes for a fine whittler if you want it."

"Thanks," Lizzie said, and accepted the gift.

Grainger turned to the sound of clopping hooves outside and saw two riders out the window coming down the street.

"Who are they?" Lizzie asked.

"They call themselves the Daltry Gang even though there's only the two brothers. The older one in the raffia straw hat and chinos is Ned. The other is Angus. He's one back-shooting son of a bitch. There's a fair price on both their heads for robbing banks and gunning down folks that got in their way."

"You going to arrest them?"

"Nope. That's a marshal's job," the bounty hunter said, tensing when the outlaws pulled back the reins and leaned on their saddle horns to appraise Selma standing by the funeral pyre.

The Daltrys conversed for a moment then Angus pulled his revolver and aimed it at Selma, who after some consideration dropped the tomahawk on the ground.

Angus threw his leg over the cantle and dismounted. He handed his horse's reins to Ned and marched over to Selma. She was standing her ground and didn't appear to be afraid of the outlaw.

"He better not hurt Momma," Lizzie hissed.

"Quiet," Grainger whispered as they watched the scene unfold outside.

Angus grabbed Selma's arm and yanked her behind him as he tramped toward the steps of the saloon. Ned got off his horse and tied their mounts to the hitching post. He followed his brother with his captive up the steps onto the planked walkway and they pushed through the batwing doors.

Grainger looked down at Lizzie. "Fetch me my boots. And when I'm gone, you're not to leave this room."

* * *

The bounty hunter strode across the dirt street, spurs clinking, and climbed the steps to the saloon. He was wearing his gun belt with the Dragoon in the holster. He had half-buttoned his shirt, leaving the top three loops undone.

He was carrying the 10-gauge Ithaca shotgun with its twin barrels.

Grainger pushed through the batwing doors and stepped inside the gloomy saloon.

The stinking remains of the dead Naguals still permeated the room and reminded him of the time he had ridden down onto a killing field of rotted carcasses after a buffalo slaughter.

He spotted the Nagual that had attempted to shapeshift into a black bear before Grainger had blasted a barrel-sized hole through its chest with the double load of silver ball bearings, spraying its heart, lungs, and innards clear across the room.

Selma had partially hacked up a corpse that lay nearby—the one halted in mid transformation as the beastly timber wolf tried to regress into its human form before the demise.

Blowflies were hovering around the blood-splattered fur, while white maggots wiggled through tiny moist tunnels of flesh.

"You kill those skin-walkers?" a gruff voice spoke from a dark corner.

Grainger turned and saw two silhouettes sitting behind a card table as the morning sun filtered through the filmy windows. "That's right."

"Never liked those Naguals. Lose the scattergun or she loses her head!"

It took a second or two for Grainger's eyes to adjust before he saw Selma.

Angus was seated beside her and had the muzzle of a .45-caliber Schofield revolver pressed against her temple.

The coach gun crashed on the floorboards.

"Now the gun belt!"

The bounty hunter suspected that Ned was slunk down, hiding behind the bar. He figured once he was disarmed, the coward would pop up like a prairie dog and commence firing.

"Have it your way," Angus said and drew back the hammer.

"I'm letting it fall." Grainger unclipped the friction buckle and his gun belt hit the floor.

"Now reach for the rafters."

Grainger lifted his arms. His shirt was sticking to the oozing bandages and he was leaking like a cask of red wine that had been used for target practice. "You can let the woman go."

"From where I'm sitting, you just lost your right to barter," Angus grumbled back.

The batwing doors burst inward and Ned stormed in, dragging Lizzie in by her hair.

"Didn't I say to stay in the room?" Grainger snapped.

"I was," Lizzie replied. "He come up and nabbed me."

"Hey, baby brother, looks like you and I are going to have ourselves some fun," Ned said.

Angus nodded his head and let out a boisterous laugh. Every tooth in his mouth was black as tar.

"Let my daughter go!" Selma's eyes narrowed with rage. The veins in her neck bulged like thick cords of rope.

Grainger could see thin trickles of blood oozing from the two puncture marks on her neck made by the honcho Nagual's fangs.

Angus saw the blood too. "What the hell? Ned, she's been bit."

Selma lowered her head. A low growl rumbled in her throat. Her shoulders hunched as she stretched her arms on the table.

She dragged her huge paws back, raking her razor-sharp claws over the tabletop, cutting deep, chiseled furrows into the wood.

Then she raised her head.

"Momma!" Lizzie screamed.

Angus' eyes widened when he realized he was sitting next to a fierce cougar. The big cat opened its mighty jaws, roared in his face, and pounced on the startled man, shoving him backward in his chair and onto the floor.

Angus let out a gurgled cry and drummed the heels of his boots on the hardwood floor as sharp teeth and claws ripped through his flesh.

Ned froze for a moment as he watched his brother being torn to bits.

The bounty hunter lowered his right hand and reached behind his head, gripping the handle of the bowie knife in the sheath strapped between his shoulder blades.

The nine-inch plus blade sailed across the room and struck the crown of Ned's straw hat with an impressive thud. He teetered then dropped to the floor with his hat pegged to his forehead.

Lizzie scampered over and hid behind Grainger.

"Please don't kill Momma," she pleaded.

The bounty hunter bent down and retrieved the shotgun, bracing himself as the carnage continued across the room in the dark corner of the saloon.

14

THE FARMSTEAD

After leaving the ghost town and riding for days, Grainger reached a bluff overlooking a canyon and saw a farmstead down below, situated near a shallow rock bed stream that meandered through the arroyo.

He assessed the shack-like clapboard farmhouse with its steep-pitched metal roof and the nearby barn, both built with similar materials by a person of limited carpentry skills. A shabby woodshed and henhouse were set in the middle of the barnyard.

Beyond was a trodden path that led through a parched brown field of wilted cornstalks to a crudely constructed privy erected at the edge of a thick stand of oaks.

Grainger searched for signs of life and saw an enormous draft mule—sixteen hands tall—standing in a section of corral, its chin resting on the top rail. It was a dark bay, mostly black with a chestnut forehead.

A behemoth Texas Longhorn bull, big as a buckboard, was in a nearby pen, its head down, snorting up dust devils. Its horns were spread seven-feet apart from tip-to-tip and were as thick as a wrangler's arms. The hide was bluish in coloring, signifying a feral ancestral lineage.

The bounty hunter figured the place was either deserted or the homesteader—if he were determined to keep trespassers off his land—was concealed down there somewhere, the site of his turkey shooter zeroed in on Grainger's head.

"We might be able to water and feed the horses," Grainger said, turning to Selma and Lizzie astride the Daltry brothers' horses.

He felt somewhat remorseful for having to tie Selma's hands to the saddle horn but he knew it had to be done.

"Let's go," he said, and turned the buckskin's head in the direction of the broad strata declivity that stretched down into the basin. Selma and Lizzie's horses followed behind the bounty hunter's mount in single file.

The horses plodded wearily down the grade.

Grainger's face was shaded under the front brim of his Stetson, his eyes wary of the first sign of trouble. He knew from his line of work that a man who paid poor attention to his surroundings only made himself a fool to the pallbearers.

As they drew nearer, Grainger noticed that the farm animals had taken a certain interest in their arrival—enough hoopla to draw an immense chanticleer out from the henhouse.

Flabbergasted, Grainger gazed upon the extraordinary bird.

The fowl was as big as a buzzard. The comb on the bridge of the crower's bony head was bright red and resembled a jagged lightning bolt. Twin wattles hung from its massive beak like two saddlebags, along with dangling earlobes.

The gamecock puffed out its plumed chest like a defiant Thanksgiving turkey and clawed the dirt with its pointy talons.

Though the farmer did not seemingly possess a talent with a hammer or a hoe, Grainger had to give him credit: the man was a wizard when it came to feed, as he surely knew how to fatten up his livestock.

Grainger rode up short of the front porch. "Hello inside! Could you spare some water for our horses?" He leaned on his saddle horn and waited for a reply.

"Could be he's in the barn," Selma said, as her horse and Lizzie's horse stopped in front of the hitching post.

"Momma, I need to use the facilities," Lizzie begged, squirming in her saddle.

"Then you better run along. Outhouse is yonder by those trees."

Lizzie scooted down off her horse and hit the ground running, her long riding skirt flapping against her skinny legs as she dashed across the barnyard and down the path toward the privy nestled by the woods.

Grainger dismounted, the reins draped on the buckskin's neck. He stared up at Selma with an apologetic expression on his weathered face. "Let me check inside before I get you down."

Selma nodded and sat solemnly in the saddle.

The bounty hunter's spurs jingled as he climbed the steps onto the porch. He pounded once on the door with his gloved fist and the hinges creaked as the door swung inward a few inches.

Brushing the front of his long coat aside, he drew the Dragoon.

"We are riders, seeking water for our horses. Nothing else, I assure you."

Grainger placed his hand on the face of the door and pushed it open, allowing the morning sunlight to illuminate the dark interior.

A thick layer of dust covered the broken-down furniture and cobwebs hung everywhere like thin-thread silver doilies. It was obvious that the place was deserted and had been abandoned for some time.

If that was so, then why were there—

Something large in frame prowled in the shadows just inside the doorway to another room.

"Show yourself and I won't shoot."

He could hear it shuffling and rubbing its body up against the other side of the wall. Whatever it was, the creature was big. And when he heard it growl, he knew with a great amount of certainty that it was tensing up its muscles getting ready for the kill.

* * *

Lizzie sprinted toward the outhouse, boots crunching across the shriveled field of corn. Upon reaching the privy, she swung open the door and quickly stepped inside. A crescent moon-shaped opening had been carved high up on the plank of wood, so even though it was dark, there was sufficient light when she closed the door, enough for her to see and wish she had chosen the woods to relieve herself instead.

The inside of the privy was teeming with labyrinth webs of preying spiders and crawling bugs clinging to the claustrophobic walls and dangling from the ceiling.

She speedily reached down and hiked up her dress. Glancing back, she spotted the box frame over the pothole and sat down.

Nasty, vile things wiggled and squirmed in the decayed defecation down in the crapper pit. She held her nose and quickly did her constitutional.

Lizzie discovered a few brittle pages of an old Sears Roebuck catalog that had been left in a rusted can and tore a page out, crinkling it to make it softer, and got the deed done. She jumped up, letting the heavy material of her skirt drop, the hem touching the tops of her bootstraps.

She pushed open the door and stepped out into the fresh air and was about to scurry back to the farmhouse when she heard a horse whinny somewhere back in the woods and thought perhaps it had strayed from the property and might be lost. She was certain if she retrieved the farmer's horse, he would be so grateful and generous enough to reward them with a hot meal and even perhaps a real bed to sleep in.

She followed the sound, which took her deeper into the copse of oaks. Soon, she saw the markings on the flank of a horse behind some brush. It was an Appaloosa. Then she saw another horse with similar spots. She came across two more horses, a palomino and a pinto. The Indian ponies were adorned with war paint and were tethered side by side to a long rope stretched and secured between two trees.

Lizzie turned and ran back the way she had come. Jutting branches scratched her face and arms as she dashed madly through the woods.

Finally out of the trees, she raced through the decomposing cornfield, waving her arms, screaming, "Momma! Momma! The Naguals are here!"

* * *

When Selma heard Lizzie yell, her horse's ears pricked forward. The animal snorted and turned its head toward the corral. And then Selma's horse spooked and sidestepped away from the pen.

Selma saw the paddock gate swing open.

The Texas Longhorn bull bolted out with its head down and charged Lizzie's horse, driving a horn tip deep between the dun's shoulder and girth, spearing the leather saddle. The bovine pulled back to free its horn and thick blood spurted out of the gored hole like a red pressure-released geyser.

Mortally wounded, the horse backed up and staggered. Its back legs gave out and it collapsed dead on its side in a crimson pool, eyes glazed and its tongue in the dirt.

The triumphant bull snorted and raised its right front hoof and stomped the ground.

Grainger's buckskin took off and galloped around the far side of the farmhouse.

Panic seized Selma and she reached for the reins in hopes of escape—but she couldn't, her hands were tied to the saddle horn.

And that is when the draft mule bounded out of the corral, calculated its attack, and with both hind hooves kicked, striking the gaskin and snapping the thigh bone and delivering an organ-imploding blow to the barrel of Selma's horse, narrowly missing her leg booted in the stirrups, leaving Selma no recourse but to hang on for dear life.

* * *

Lizzie had never seen a giant rooster before.

But there it was.

Standing in her path.

It was as tall as her, staring with beady eyes that reminded her of black marbles.

The head kept bobbing up and down like it had a disorder. The gamecock was not distracted by the clamor made by the horses and the livestock in front of the farmhouse.

Its sole focus was on Lizzie.

Lizzie reached inside the pocket of her skirt.

The rooster leaped in the air, scattering feathers as it flapped its wings and flew at Lizzie with its sharp spurs pointed at her face.

* * *

Grainger stood motionless, ignoring the ruckus outside as his attention was on the phantom lurking just inside the other room. The bizarre noises emanating from the room had been chilling—like sodden branches snapping, accompanied by fitful moans.

He pointed the long barrel of his Dragoon and approached the doorway.

As he advanced, he heard the distinct ratchet sound of a lever-action inserting a cartridge into the chamber.

The Nagual stepped out of the shadows. He was wearing traditional Indian garb: cloth headband, cotton shirt hanging over pants tucked inside the tops of knee-high leather boots. He was no longer in the body of his spiritual animal-self but in human form, so that he might use his Winchester to get the drop on the bounty hunter.

Grainger fired first.

The headshot made by the .44-caliber slug cleaved a teacup-sized chunk of skull out of the Nagual's cranium, brain matter exploding in a gory mist.

Suddenly, the whole farmhouse shook when the front door and adjacent walls smashed into kindling and the Texas Longhorn trampled in and charged Grainger.

With the grace of a rodeo performer, the bounty hunter grabbed a hold of the right horn and swung up on the animal's shoulders as the bull stormed through the farmhouse and crashed out the rear wall, upending Grainger and spilling him across the barnyard.

The bull spun around, narrowing its eyes on its prey.

Grainger gazed up with relief when the buckskin appeared and trotted over, allowing him to reach behind the saddle's bedroll and pull out the coach gun as the aggressive Longhorn charged.

He waited for the bull to get within five feet and fired both barrels.

The head burst in a grisly cloud as it disintegrating between the horns, wet slabs of meat flying everywhere as the headless brute plunged onto the dirt.

* * *

Before her horse could hit the ground, Selma changed into the cougar. The metamorphoses had been that quick. This time her fear had triggered the transformation where before it had been anger. Perhaps to her animal spiritual self they were the same.

Clinging to the saddle, she arched her back and when the draft mule was in range, she lunged.

The animal whimpered as she buried her sharp claws into its shoulders and back.

She raked the withers with her right paw, ripping deep slashes down its hide.

Refusing to be bucked off, she sank her teeth into the back of the neck, biting and grinding her teeth until she snapped the spinal cord.

She leaped off as the mule's legs buckled and it dropped.

* * *

The airborne rooster smacked into Lizzie, knocking her down on the ground. She raised her forearm over her face to ward off the bird's repetitive pecking as it tried to gouge out her eyes. The bird's weight pressed on her thighs and she could feel the talons digging into the rawhide material, attempting to rip her skirt and tear at her flesh.

Lizzie came up with her left hand and stabbed the rooster in the chest with the penny knife but the blade was too small to render serious injury. So she plunged the blade in again and again.

Blood began to drench over her but the wounds she was inflicting only seemed to make the gamecock angrier and did nothing to lessen the voracity of the assault and she knew she would not be the victor.

But that all changed when the 120-pound cougar bit off the rooster's head and stomped its body to the dirt, thrashing it apart with its claws, feathers flying about the barnyard as if a prankster had blown up a down pillow with a stick of dynamite.

The big cat's face and body were smeared with blood as it turned, standing only five feet away.

"Momma?" Lizzie said as she peered into the deep-set emerald eyes.

Heavy boots approached.

Lizzie glanced up and saw Grainger trudging over, plucking two spent shells out of the coach gun's breeches, and inserting fresh cartridges.

"Please! No!" Lizzie yelled.

The cougar reared back, bared its fangs, and hissed at the bounty hunter.

Grainger raised the shotgun and swung the barrel, clipping the animal on the side of the head, and knocking it unconscious.

He looked down at Lizzie and half grinned. "Your momma's going to be mighty sore at me when she wakes up."

* * *

With torch in hand, Grainger went about setting fire to the strewed chunks. He figured the rooster Nagual had been a dwarf. Small flaming mounds littered the barnyard.

The bounty hunter had dragged the Nagual out of the farmhouse and piled it with the headless bull. The skin-walker that had been the mule had died a slow and agonizing death, allowing it to mutate back to human form before its spirit left to travel to some hellish place.

Grainger torched the heap and threw the burning branch into the inferno. The Daltrys' horses were not cursed and did not need cremation so he left them to the scavengers.

Selma and Lizzie sat on the saddled Appaloosas and watched as the dark smoke rose from the crackling fires. Grainger had set both the palomino and the pinto free.

He strode over, lifted his boot into the stirrup, and climbed into the saddle. He pulled on the split reins, tugging the snaffle bit in the buckskin's mouth, and turned the horse around.

Selma faced him, a light bruise on her cheek. She held out her hands, the insides of her wrists pressed together, a prisoner waiting to be bound.

"Let's see how it goes," Grainger said, and smiled when he saw the woman and the child's eyes brighten.

And with that, the bounty hunter spurred his horse and the three galloped up the steep incline toward the bluff and the vast badlands beyond.

15

THE SNAKEMEN

After a blistering trek crossing a salt flat, Grainger suggested they make camp for the night at the base of a talus near a rocky draw. A large pocket between the boulders provided adequate shelter on the chance a windstorm kicked up while they slept.

He'd removed the Daltry brothers' saddles from the Appaloosas, the rugged horses having taken to the heavier rigging just fine even though they were accustomed to the Naguals' way, who used lighter hides and blankets when riding their Indian ponies.

The ground was too dense to drive a stake for a tether, so Grainger bound both horses' front hooves with leather twist hobbles so they couldn't wander off and bolt; the buckskin he left unshackled, knowing his steed was not prone to ambling.

While Grainger laid out the saddles and bedrolls, Selma and Lizzie went off to comb the barren terrain for anything ignitable. Their search drew them farther away from the campsite, as the pickings were sparse.

Selma came upon a knee-high sage down by the gully bank. She grabbed the stalk to pull it out of the hard-cracked clay, and even though the skeletal bush was withered, the roots were anchored firmly as though clutching to the earth's core. She yanked, first one-handed, then with both but to no avail. With no other recourse, Selma snatched the tomahawk tucked in her belt, raised the sharp blade and with a single swing, chopped the shrubby plant down. She snapped the branches for kindling and put the remnants in a canvas tote.

"Momma, come see."

Selma traipsed over and saw her daughter pointing at an arch of metal butting out of the compact clay.

"It's a wagon wheel," Selma said. She knelt and used the tomahawk as a spade to dig but the ground was hard as granite. "Shame, we could have burned the spokes."

"Think these folks died here?" Lizzie asked.

"No telling." Selma rose and gazed farther up the dried creek bed. "Let's see where this goes."

On their way they saw signs that the route had been journeyed before by other travelers as they came across things such as a metal ribbing of a

Conestoga, a sun-bleached boot, the upper skeletal half of a mule, a shredded parasol, an empty steamer trunk, and a few unexplainable particulars sticking out of the ground.

They trudged on, reaching a rocky path. Soon the shale became a gravelly trail for a spell, ending at a flatland of sand.

Lizzie stopped abruptly and grabbed her mother's hand. "Are those..."

There were sandy mounds that looked to be a crude burial site, only the graves were half the length considered for a normal sized person. The plots were haphazardly placed, each one with a burrow hole at one end, cavernous enough to shove a powder keg down inside.

"Look Momma." Lizzie pointed at a narrow rut stretching across the sand.

"Oh my Lord," Selma gasped when she saw the strange impressions on either side of the furrow.

"Those aren't footprints."

"No, they're not. They're handprints."

"You don't think that someone was crawling in the sand?" Lizzie said.

Selma studied the peculiar mounds, wondering what might have made them. She had an uneasy feeling. "Let's go back. I think I can break up that steamer trunk with the axe, get us enough wood for a good fire."

"Sure thing, Momma."

* * *

After arriving at the campsite, Selma stowed the filled canvas tote by the fire pit ringed with rocks that Grainger had arranged while they were gone.

Grainger was knelt over his open bedroll, delving through his saddlebag. "I know I got some pemmican in here somewhere."

Selma and Lizzie sat down opposite the bounty hunter and watched him pull out a silver-plated Forehand & Wadsworth pocket revolver and two boxes of .31-caliber cartridges for the double-action five-shooter. He took out a fistful of gun parts, an over-under double-barreled .41-caliber Remington derringer, and then a tied leather bundle of throwing knives.

Exasperated, he lifted the saddlebag and turned it upside-down, impatiently dumping the remaining contents including a cloth sack that fell out amongst the deluge of shotgun shells and other artifacts privy to a bounty hunter's trade.

"It's not a porterhouse but it's the best I got," Grainger said, unknotting the string and opening the bag. He handed Selma and Lizzie each a cured bison strip that could have easily been mistaken for a tongue cut out of an old boot.

"Thanks," Lizzie said and bit down on the stiff jerky. She gnawed the tough meat, grinding her molars, switching over and using the row of teeth on the other side of her mouth but was still unable to chew. She looked up at Grainger, who was smiling back at her like he had just heard a knee-slapping joke.

"You best suck on that awhile," he chuckled. "Soften it up if you don't want to be a toothless granny."

"But I'm hungry," Lizzie replied.

"Your spit will trick your belly."

It was close to nightfall as the sun fell into the horizon—molten steel returning to the cauldron—and the sky bruised a purplish black.

"I'll build a fire." Grainger reached in his jean pocket and removed a small tin box. He popped off the lid, and inside were a tuff of dried lichen and two flints. He shifted over to the canvas tote and grabbed a handful of sage branches. He broke them in two, and formed a teepee in the center of the fire pit. He crumbled up some dried twigs and shoved them inside the cone's base then added a pinch of lichen from the tin. Taking the two flints, he leaned forward and struck them together repeatedly, each time creating a spark. Soon the lichen caught and there was promising smoke, then a tiny flame.

The fire crept up the teepee like a rumba of red rattlers.

Grainger reached over and grabbed a few strips of flat wood embedded with brass tacks from the canvas tote. "Where'd you find these?"

"Over by the gully," Selma said. "Near some sand mounds."

Grainger gave her a curious look.

"We also found a strange trail. Handprints in the sand."

The bounty hunter stood and drew his Dragoon.

Selma and Lizzie looked up with concern.

"What are they?" Selma asked.

"Snakemen."

"But that's only an Indian legend."

"I've heard it said that they used to be real men," Grainger said as he began his tale. "It's been told that a group of settlers passing through were set upon by a band of Naguals. The Naguals stole the women and children and left the men to die in the desert. That's when a Nagual medicine man cast a curse and turned them into snakemen, banishing them to live underground. The only time they come to the surface is to appease their vengeful souls on unsuspecting travelers, much like ourselves."

Grainger stared out between the boulders at the barren landscape stretching for miles. He saw no sign of life, not even a cactus, just a darkening, desolate wasteland.

"And you believe that?" Selma asked.

"If you heard it different, I'd be obliged to listen."

Selma shook her head.

Grainger glanced over at the weary horses; their heads drooped, flanks pressed as they leaned against one another. They were in no condition to saddle up which meant that they had no choice but to stay put.

He turned and stared grimly at Selma and Lizzie then knelt on his bedroll.

Grainger picked up the pocket revolver and handed it to Selma. She looked at the puny gun. "I'm a farmer's wife. You can do better than that."

"Yep, I reckon I can." The bounty hunter went over to a blanket roll and untied the leather strap. He turned back the blanket revealing the Daltry brothers' firearms that he had confiscated. The dead men's guns were no longer of use to them so it wasn't like he had thieved them. He bent down and picked up the .44-caliber Winchester lever-action that had been in Ned's rifle scabbard on his saddle. "This more to your liking?" he asked.

Selma reached out with her left hand and grabbed the rifle by its long barrel, and with her right hand, ratcheted the lever-action then sighted down the barrel like a gunsmith contemplating a purchase. "This will do."

Grainger couldn't help but smile. "How about you?" he said to Lizzie.

"I can shoot," the girl replied as if asking her the question was an insult.

"Here, try this on for size." He handed Lizzie the over-under double-barreled Remington derringer.

Lizzie took the tiny gun that looked big in her hands. She hefted the weapon as if gauging its weight measured its worth. She looked up at Grainger and nodded in agreement.

"Good. Keep a mind, each barrel fires separately. Gives you two shots. A forty-one caliber is a fair load but I'd aim for the head."

"Yes sir."

"I doubt we'll be getting any sleep," Grainger said, looking weary-eyed at both Selma and Lizzie. "Snakemen only come out at night."

* * *

The encroaching night was a black beast, nibbling at the tips of the campfire flames as the snakemen slithered in the sand under the veil of darkness.

"So those belongings we saw back at the gulch, those were from wagon train folks that got ambushed by these snakemen?" Selma asked.

"That would be my guess." Grainger said, and slipped on the bandolier stuffed with 10-gauge shells. He snapped open the chamber on the coach gun and fed two loads.

Grainger stood with the Ithaca ready, his Dragoon in the holster, the Navy Colt tucked in his gun belt next to his sheathed bowie knife; Selma on his right, the barrel of the Winchester resting on the crook of her arm; Lizzie to his left, holding the derringer with both hands.

"Selma, you keep the rear watch if they should come down those rocks behind us."

A snakeman came out of the darkness, visible in the faint light. Its chalk-white head was oval with no facial features; it had shoulders and arms with hands like that of a man but then its body tapered into a thick ten-foot long serpent tail.

"My God, it has no face," Selma said.

"It doesn't look that tough," Lizzie said, raising the derringer.

"Careful what you say, little girl," Grainger said.

While they had been conversing, the snakeman had been tilting its head in their direction as if it were eavesdropping even though it had no ears, perhaps drawn by vibrations instead of actual language.

The snakeman suddenly shot across the sand, clawing the ground with its hands and propelling itself with its powerful swishing tail.

Lizzie fired. The bullet struck the snakeman in the chest but still it kept coming.

Grainger blasted the thing with buckshot and stopped it dead in its tracks.

Another snakeman had slithered between the rocks and was attacking the horses. Clutching an Appaloosa's leg, it pulled itself up, grappling until it snatched the mane and wrapped its strong tail around the horse's neck. Taut muscles constricted in a hangman's noose as the horse struggled to stay on its feet.

The buckskin charged in and champed down on the snakeman's arm. The tombstone teeth bit hard enough that the creature released its death grip on the Appaloosa. Grainger's steed shook its head and upended the snakeman so that it landed on the ground. The horse reared up and came down with its mighty front hooves like iron pistons, crushing the snakeman's skull.

Selma shot a snakeman as it came down the rocks. She levered another cartridge in the chamber, aimed the Winchester, and, like a champion marksman at a turkey shoot, picked off another creature glissading over a boulder.

Grainger blasted another snakeman. He dropped his coach gun rather than reload, and pulled out his Dragoon and Navy Colt. He popped off a few well-aimed shots, each slug hitting its intended mark.

Selma felt a tight grip on her ankle and was yanked off her feet. The rifle flew from her hands. She landed facedown and immediately got on her hands and knees and spun around to confront her assailant. The snakeman grabbed her by the throat with both hands and wrapped its crushing tail around her midsection. She could feel the air squeezing from her lungs, her ribs compressing like a thin-walled pail under the weight of an anvil.

She stared into the blank face. Up close, it was hideous and looked like a skin-tight hood that had been soaked and starched in white flour and left to dry. Before her last breath was forced out of her, Lizzie turned into her animal-self.

Her cougar body bulged against the coiling snakeman's tail, breaking its hold enough that she could squirm free. She sunk her fangs into the snakeman's neck and savagely tore out the flesh. The creature thrashed and writhed in a dramatic death throe, and after a few paroxysm jerks, drew still in the crimson sand.

Selma stood over her kill to make sure it was dead. She heard the horses whinny briefly and then all went still and quiet around the campsite. She closed her eyes, ruminated for a moment, and reverted back to her human-self. She got to her feet and staggered over to where Grainger and Lizzie stood by the campfire.

"Have they gone?" she asked.

"They've had their fill," Grainger said. "I suggest you two get some rest."

"What about you?" Selma asked.

"I'll stay up, tend to the fire."

"Any inclination where we might be going?" Selma looked pensively at Grainger as she steered Lizzie toward the bedrolls.

"There's a town half a day's ride from here."

"Is it a good place?"

"No. I don't think the devil himself would live there."

"Then why are we going?"

"There're some very bad men there with a big bounty on their heads."

"And you aim to collect," Selma said, slipping under her blanket and resting her head back on the stiff saddle serving as a poor excuse for a pillow.

"Yes, ma'am."

16

THE RAPACIOUS GANG

They arrived the next afternoon and tied up their horses behind a boardinghouse at the edge of town. Grainger led the way through the backdoor. The place was as quiet as an abandoned mine as they entered the small parlor.

"Where is everyone?" Selma said, glancing about the room meant as a gathering place for socializing: a pair of matching armchairs, a rocker, and a chesterfield positioned in front of the stone hearth.

Lizzie stood at the double-door entry that led into the dining room. "Are we going to eat in here?" She turned and smiled, her face unable to contain her excitement.

"I'd say it's time you two had some home cooking." Grainger spotted a secretary desk with the front panel open. Dangling from hooks was a row of keys with assigned room numbers. He took one and handed it to Selma.

"Go make yourselves at home. I'll settle up with the proprietor later."

"Hope they have a bath," Selma said, then narrowed her eyes on the bounty hunter. "Where will you be?"

"Paying a visit to the sheriff."

"You be careful."

Grainger grinned. "I'll do my best."

"Good. See that you do."

* * *

After Grainger had brought the bedrolls and saddlebags into the room, he left Selma and Lizzie at the boardinghouse and led the horses by the reins past the rear of the buildings, as he didn't want his presence to be known. He found a corral behind a livery stable. He ushered the horses into the pen. He unbuckled their saddle straps and took off the rigging. The Appaloosas trod over to the water trough while the buckskin grazed on an alfalfa bale.

Grainger walked around to the main street and thought that it was unusual that there were no townspeople to be seen. He saw the Sheriff's Office and ambled over. He opened the door and stepped inside.

"Can I help you?" the man behind the desk asked. His right shirtsleeve was folded up and pinned to his shoulder.

"You the sheriff?"

"In a matter of speaking."

The bounty hunter reached under his slicker, pulled out a wanted poster, and flattened it on the desk. "I'm here for these men."

"They aren't men," the sheriff snarled.

Grainger motioned to the sheriff's missing arm. "They do that to you?"

"That's right."

"Then I'd say you got off easy."

"You think it's easy for a one-armed man to keep the law without his gun hand?"

"I'm saying it could have been worse. The Rapacious Gang has a proclivity for human flesh."

"Damn cannibals made me watch while they ate my arm."

"Why'd they stop there?" asked Grainger.

"So I'd sit here. Lure strangers like you to them."

The bounty hunter gave the sheriff a contemptible look.

"But I never done it, I swear. You're the first new face I've seen in weeks."

"Then I guess you won't mind if I claim the reward?"

"Mister, there're four of them."

"I know." Grainger took a moment to look out the window. "Doesn't anyone live here?"

"Most everyone run off," the sheriff said in a pitiful tone. "The ones that stayed they kidnapped. Took them to their abattoir."

"And where would that be?"

"The boardinghouse."

* * *

"When I come back, you're getting in next."

"But Momma, can't I just clean up here?" Lizzie protested, pointing at the flowery-designed porcelain washbasin on the bedside table.

"Quit your fussing and hush," Selma said, and stepped out of the room and closed the door.

Wearing only a slip and carrying a towel, Selma walked barefoot down the carpet toward the opened door at the end of the hall where she could see a portion of a lion claw tub. She had never bathed in such elegance before. On the farm, Jonathan had jury-rigged an outdoor shower behind the barn with a swiveling barrel that dowsed ice-cold water whenever the bather tugged on a rope. She looked forward to slipping into that fancy tub and languishing in fragrant bath salts.

When she was only a few feet from the door, she noticed that there was a hallway to the right with more doors to other rooms. Someone moaned from behind one of those doors.

"Hello?" Selma turned and stepped down the hallway.

She heard groaning, and a person sobbing, each from a different room.

A door had been left ajar.

Selma peered inside. A naked man was trussed to a bed. He was groaning with his eyes closed. His left wrist was bound to a brass headboard; his right arm and legs had been reduced to cauterized stumps.

"Oh my God," Selma gasped and stepped back.

Another door swung open. A man with a greasy ponytail beard stood in the threshold. His bare chest and arms were caked with dried blood. He wore a baggy pair of grimy trousers and his bare feet were filthy. He took one look at Selma and pulled out a 10-inch pig sticker.

Selma spun on her heels and ran toward the junction in the hall. She had to get back to the room before they found Lizzie.

A second man was blocking the hall. He wore a ragged pair of red long johns and a two-holster rig around his waist with the handgrips of his revolvers facing forward.

"Get out of my way!" Selma glared at the man.

She looked to her left and saw the other man stepping out of the room, followed by another man carrying a machete. They were spitting images of each other and were surely twins.

And then she saw a fourth man.

Opening the door to her and Lizzie's room.

A sinewy arm came from behind and clamped around Selma's throat.

She was dragged into the bathing room and flung to the floor next to the lion claw tub. She looked up and saw the twin with the machete. He closed the door and locked it with a key and stood there, staring at her, smiling shamelessly with a mouthful of rotted teeth.

* * *

"I'm coming Momma," Lizzie said when she heard the door opening. She was sitting on the edge of the bed with her back to the door, untying her boots. She raised her boot and with the toe of her other shoe, pushed the heel down and pulled out her stocking foot. She looked over her shoulder...

An ugly man with wily hair and a slobbered beard stood at the door. He was naked except for a codpiece over his groin, covering his man parts. He stared at Lizzie and tittered like a simpleton.

He raised a cudgel he'd been holding by his side. The bloodstained club looked like a butcher's mallet.

The man stepped into the room.

Lizzie dove to the floor and scrambled under the bed, dragging a saddlebag behind her.

The man lunged on the bed. His sudden weight pushed the mattress down, bowing the wooden slats.

Lizzie scooted under to the middle of the bed. She flipped open the flap and frantically rummaged inside the saddlebag.

The mattress flew up from the bed and was tossed across the room.

The man gazed down through the wooden slats.

Lizzie pointed the pocket revolver up through an opening and tugged on the trigger.

The bullet tore off his right ear. Instead of hollering from the excruciating pain, the strange man cackled like a demented hag. A runnel of blood leaked out the side of his head and ran down his neck and shoulder. He put his hand up to the wound. He looked at the blood on his fingers. Then he licked each digit like he was savoring the taste of a delicious sauce.

Lizzie fired a second shot.

A scarlet mist burst from his ruptured heart as the slug punched through his sternum.

He hung like a dark cloud then came crashing down.

The bed broke apart and collapsed on top of her.

Lying there, pinned under the dead man, Lizzie wished she hadn't been so stubborn about taking a bath and had gone with her mother.

* * *

Grainger entered through the front door and stormed into the boardinghouse with his guns drawn. He strode through the sitting room to the first hallway. He could hear murmurs and scuffling behind a door to one of the rooms.

Tucking the Dragoon in the holster so he would have a free hand, he reached down for the knob, pointed the Navy Colt, and opened the door.

Two naked men with gags and kerchief blindfolds were hogtied on the floor.

“Good Lord,” Grainger muttered. He pulled out his bowie knife, went over, and cut the first man free who was lying facedown with his wrists bound to his ankles.

The man stretched out his legs, turned over, and sat up. He reached up and tore off the blindfold and pulled the cloth out of his mouth. “Much obliged to you,” he said to Grainger.

The bounty hunter cut the other man loose and removed his blindfold. The man sat up and spat out the rag. Rubbing the rope burns on his wrists, he too thanked his rescuer.

“I’d suggest you two hightail it out the window.”

The men got to their feet on wobbly legs. They each grabbed a piece of bedding and wrapped it around their nakedness.

Grainger opened the window and watched as they scrambled out one at a time, falling over one another as they made the drop.

Leaving the room, Grainger continued down the corridor until he reached a bend that led to another hallway where he saw what looked like an old prospector wearing a pair of red long johns and a gun belt. He had his forearms crossed in front of his groin. Judging by his bedraggled appearance, Grainger doubted the man was modest. Which meant only one thing. He was wearing his guns backwards.

The man whipped his revolvers up but before he could get off a single round, Grainger fired his Navy Colt and shot him in the forehead.

His head jerked back and his body followed, six-shooters scattering as he landed on the floor.

Grainger heard a rush of footsteps come up from behind, and then a sharp pain in his shoulder blade. He felt the cold steel ripped from his flesh. He turned and saw a man that looked like a trapper with a ponytail beard standing with a long-shank knife, blood dripping off the blade.

The wild man thrust the knife again, slashing Grainger’s forearm, causing him to drop his gun. Now with the advantage over an unarmed opponent, the man lunged again but this time the bounty hunter sidestepped the attack and plunged his bowie knife between the other man’s ribs, twisting the handle. The man fell against the wall and slid to the floor.

Grainger stumbled down the hall until he came to an opened doorway. He looked inside and saw a man without clothes sprawled on top of a smashed bed frame.

“Help.”

“Lizzie?”

"I'm under here."

Grainger staggered into the room. With his good arm he was able to roll the dead man off. He reached down and pulled Lizzie up out of the rubble.

"Where's your ma?"

"She went to take a bath."

"Then we best find her."

They went out of the room and hurried down the hallway to the bathing room.

Grainger tried the doorknob. It was locked so he kicked in the door.

A man was lying in a lion claw tub with one leg draped over the side. His head was lulled back. The ponytail beard was matted with blood and pasted inside his masticated throat. His chest had been torn open and was raked with deep claw marks.

Grainger had to do a double take as the man looked exactly like the one he had just killed a few minutes ago.

He noticed a machete lying on the floor.

"Selma? Are you in here?"

As if to reply, a long yellow tail appeared from behind the base of the tub and uncoiled on the floor.

"Momma!"

The tail responded with a wag.

"What say we give her a minute," Grainger said. He ushered Lizzie out and closed the door.

* * *

Grainger sat in another man's rocker in the cool evening breeze and stared out at the flat, stony plain with outcrops of rocks and scattered cacti. The front door creaked open and Selma stepped out carrying two mugs of coffee. She handed one to Grainger then sat in the porch swing.

"A man could get used to this," he told her and sipped his coffee.

"You know as well as I do as soon as you're healed you'll be riding out."

Grainger stared down at the top of his mug. "I put the farm in your name."

"I hope you didn't have to spend all your bounty money."

"Nope, just enough to change the name on the title, seeing as the Rapacious Gang ate—" Grainger cleared his throat and continued by saying "—killed the man who owned this place."

Lizzie came running around the side of the farmhouse and raced up the porch steps. A shaggy dog came charging right behind.

"Who might this be?" Grainger said as the mongrel came up to him and nuzzled its nose on his lap.

"I'm calling him Scraps," Lizzie said and flopped next to her mother on the swing.

"Well, that's a...mighty fine name," Grainger laughed. He looked over at the woman and the young girl and felt something swelling inside his chest that he had never felt before. He raised his mug to Selma and she raised hers.

His back was sore, so he leaned back gingerly in the rocker, watching the sun setting slowly on the horizon. The purplish sky was minutes away from full darkness, casting shadows across the chaparral basin for miles between the bordering bluffs and twin buttes in the distance.

17

TALE'S END

"And so now you know something about your great-great grandmother," Camilla said to Sophia. Everyone was silent; the only sound the constant clinking of the night bugs bouncing off the globe of the porch light.

Miguel and Maria watched their daughter, waiting for Sophia's reaction as she gazed about the porch and stared out at the desert. "Abuela?"

"Yes, child," Camilla answered.

"Is this the same house as in the story?"

"It sure is. Been in the family for generations. That rocker you're sitting in is the same one Grainger sat in that very night."

Sophia glanced down at the chair with a new admiration. She looked up at Camilla with a questioning expression on her face. "Was that really true?"

"Why of course, child."

Sophia looked to her father.

Miguel shrugged and gave her a smile.

"Really, shapeshifters and snakemen?" Sophia said skeptically.

Camilla smiled at her granddaughter. "You'd be surprised what's out there."

Sophia still didn't look convinced. Before she could say more, a lone coyote's howl pierced the night from somewhere out in the desert.

"Let's you and I go inside so your dad can spend some time with Abuela," Maria said to Sophia, slipping off the porch swing and taking Miguel's empty glass. She grabbed the empty pitcher off the deck.

Sophia propelled herself from the rocker. She brought her glass and collected Camilla's, who smiled appreciatively.

Maria opened the screen door and the two entered the house.

After a moment, Miguel looked at his mother who was staring pensively at the whitish clouds in the otherwise star-studded sky. "Why have you waited so long before telling Sophia about Lizzy?"

"I wasn't sure if she would believe it," Camilla replied.

"If it makes you feel any better, I've always been a believer."

"Spoken like a true cryptid hunter."

"Yeah, well, don't forget I'm also the son of a great storyteller."

PART THREE

DESERT HEAT

18

BRAWL

After pulling a late shift at the convenience store, Macy was dog-tired. She knew she should go home, check up on her boys, but she wanted to see Ethan and guessed he was probably at the Mesa. She normally didn't like to go there so late at night as that is when the undesirables frequented the place, but she figured she would be safe as long as Ethan was there.

It was close to midnight by the time she pulled into the parking lot along with a dozen beat up cars and pickups, and two Harley-Davidson motorcycles parked under a floodlight. A big rig was on the edge of the lot adjacent to the highway.

She got out of her car and walked across the gravelly tarmac to the bar's front door.

As soon as she stepped inside the gloomy establishment she could smell the rank stink of men's sweat, commingled with cigarette smoke and stale beer. Her eyes watered and she coughed to clear her throat. She was tempted to turn around and leave.

She felt sorry for the bartender having to breathe in the foul air for an entire shift but it was just another occupational hazard, as she well knew, just like any other job.

Two men, and an elderly couple that were pretty much permanent fixtures, sat at the bar. Half a dozen were scattered about the tables, with a few more regulars hunkered in the booths.

Billiard balls clacked on the pool table in the back.

Macy took a moment to adjust her eyes to the dark, and then spotted Ethan sitting with his head hung down, alone at a table across the room. The tabletop was cluttered with empty beer bottles, a shot glass lying on its side, and a pint of J&B that Ethan must have smuggled in.

She strolled over, pulled out a chair, and sat across from him. He was either passed-out drunk or he hadn't heard her, she wasn't sure. "I see you started without me," Macy said. She poured herself a shot of scotch whiskey from the pint bottle and downed it in one gulp.

Ethan raised his head slowly. He looked her in the face and smiled. "Sorry. Sometimes I can't stop myself."

"I know." Macy refilled the shot glass.

"Buy you a drink?"

"You already did," Macy replied and threw back the shot.

"I thought I'd find you here," boomed a deep baritone voice.

Macy looked up and saw Ethan's brother, Kane, walking up to their table.

"Come on. Let's go," he said.

"I'm not going anywhere," Ethan said. "I'm fine right where I am."

"Get up!" Kane grabbed Ethan by the arm.

"Off me!" Ethan yelled, pulling his arm free.

"Why don't you let him be?" Macy said.

Kane gave her an evil stare. Even in the dim light, she could see his piercing eyes; unpredictable like a wild animal.

"Mind your own business," Kane said.

"No. We're sitting here having a drink. Now go and leave us alone."

"Maybe you didn't hear me." Kane backhanded the pint bottle with such force that it went flying across the room and knocked the drinks off of a table where two bikers were sitting. They bolted to their feet and kicked back their chairs.

The men had scraggly beards and wore heavy denim jackets with cutoff sleeves, crusty jeans, and black motorcycle boots. The tall one had greasy black shoulder-length hair; the shorter biker bald as a cue ball. Prison tats covered their muscular arms most likely buffed from prison yard workouts and they looked tough enough to be a World Wrestling Federation tag team.

"You got a problem?" said the tall biker.

"This doesn't concern you," Kane said.

"It does when you start throwing shit our way," the other biker said. He pulled a long blade hunting knife from a sheath on his belt.

"You boys take it outside," the bartender said, "or I'm calling the sheriff."

"Let's go, Ethan," Kane said.

Ethan looked at the two big men then turned to his brother. "I don't think so."

"See what you've done?" Macy said, glaring up at Kane.

"This asshole bothering you?" the tall biker asked, looking for any excuse to start busting heads.

"Yeah, as a matter of fact," Macy said. She looked over at Ethan and saw a strange look come over his face.

"Next time, when I tell you to mind your own business, do as I say," Kane said and kicked the side of Macy's chair, knocking her over onto the floor.

"Damn it, Kane." Ethan jumped up from the table.

The bikers took that as their invitation to brawl.

The one with the knife came at Ethan.

Ethan flipped the table onto its side, spilling the bottles onto the floor. He reached down, grabbed two beer bottles by the bottoms and smashed the necks together, shattering the ends into jagged edged weapons.

The short biker swung the sharp blade at Ethan's face. Ethan ducked, and like a prizefighter landing multiple body blows, stabbed the biker repeatedly in the chest and belly with the broken beer bottles. Patches of blood bloomed on the front of the man's thick denim jacket. He took a step back, dropped his knife, and fell against a table.

The tall biker charged Kane. Even though he outweighed Kane by a hundred pounds and was six inches taller, Kane stood his ground.

Grabbing Kane by the shirt, the biker reared back with his fist, but before he could throw a punch, Kane grabbed the man's fingers clutching his shirt, and with one quick motion, snapped all four digits back with a loud crack.

The tall biker let out a terrible scream.

Kane gave him something to really scream about and jabbed the man's right eye with a sharp thumb thrust.

Macy heard what she thought was a fierce dog, and for a moment wondered if maybe the bartender had sent in his Rottweiler from the backroom to break up the fight.

She could see Ethan hunched in the shadows behind the tipped-over table. The noise was coming from him. He was scratching at the hardwood floor with his nails and growling like a mad dog.

Kane went over and grabbed Ethan, making sure his brother kept his head down so no one could see his face, and started to usher him toward the front door. Looking over his shoulder, Kane's parting words to Macy were, "This is all your doing," and escorted Ethan out of the bar.

Macy watched the two hardcore bikers lick their wounds.

The tall biker cradled his injured hand in the pocket of his denim jacket, cupping his right eye with his other hand. The short biker opened up his denim jacket and gazed at the dozen stab wounds to his torso, which even though there was blood, the punctures didn't seem deep. He picked up his knife and slipped it back into his belt.

Neither said anything and walked out the door.

The bartender came out from behind the bar. He up-righted the table, put the chairs back in place, and picked up the strewn bottles like nothing had happened.

Everyone went back to nursing their drinks.

For Macy, it was time to go home.

19

LECHUGILLA

Vera watched Felix carefully pack her recent paintings. Once a month the packaging specialist would make a trip down from Albuquerque to pick up her artwork so her agent could post images on the gallery's website and arrange for prospective buyers.

"I especially love this one," Felix said, appreciating the canvas in his hands of a desert vista with the sun rising over a distant mountain range. He covered the painting with a sheet of glassine paper then wrapped it in bubble pack and placed it inside a protective foam inlay.

"Yes. That's one of my favorites," Vera responded, recalling the location where she had taken the photograph she had used to replicate the image with her acrylics.

Felix carried the wrapped painting over to a pushcart and slipped the artwork into a slot inside a specially designed crate. Instead of fastening the lid, he looked around the studio and said, "That's it?"

"For now," Vera replied.

"Gene was expecting one in particular."

"Really. Which one is that?"

"The lechugilla."

"It isn't ready yet."

"You haven't finished the painting?"

"I haven't even started it."

"Why not? This isn't like you."

"It's not up to me. The reason I have to wait is that this particular lechugilla hasn't been ready. It needs to fully bloom, which will be today. This plant is over twenty years old and only flowers once in its lifetime. And when it does, it dies, giving me only this narrow window of opportunity.

"Here, let me show you." Vera grabbed her digital camera from the table. She showed Felix the screen and scrolled through some pictures of the location in a box canyon and the actual plant about to be sensationalized in the art world.

"Wow, that's amazing. And Gene knows this?"

"He does. Believe me, this painting will be worth plenty once I'm done."

"Aren't you worried someone might beat you to the punch? Take pictures?"

"No. It's my little secret; no one knows where it is."

Felix fastened the lid on the crate. "So what do I tell Gene?"

"I'm going out there today."

"I don't think he'll be happy," Felix said, pushing his cart out into the hall.

"When I'm finished, I'll drive it up myself," Vera said. "Save you a trip."

"I'll let him know. Thanks, I appreciate it."

"And kindly remind him that Michelangelo didn't paint the Sistine Chapel in a day. That took four years. Tell Gene he'll have his masterpiece when I'm good and ready."

20

SADDLING UP

Astuto squatted on the porch across from Sophia while she shuffled three inverted cups in circular motions on the deck, trying to confuse the troll. He watched intently, never once taking his eyes off the swiftly moving cups.

Sophia stopped, lining the cups in a single row. "Okay, see if you can find it this time."

Astuto leaned forward. He sniffed each cup. After some determination, he lifted the third cup. There was nothing underneath.

"Ha ha," Sophia said. "Fooled you again." She lifted the middle cup, revealing a quarter coin piece. "That's the fourth time in a row I've won."

The troll looked up and pointed to Sophia's thin necklace with a topaz gem draped down the front of her neck. He repeatedly jabbed his finger at the cups and back to the necklace. Astuto patted the small wooden box by his side. He lifted the lid so Sophia could see that it was filled with more coins. He pushed the box toward Sophia.

"You want to bet all of that against my necklace?" Sophia said. "You know you're going to lose and it will all be mine. Okay." Sophia reached behind her neck and undid the clasp. She placed the jewelry under a cup. "Say goodbye to all your money."

With a quick slight of hand, Sophia moved the three cups around, doing her best to trick the troll. This time she did it twice as long as before.

Finally she stopped. "Ta-da."

Astuto sniffed the first cup, then the second. But instead of using his nose to distinguish if the third cup was indeed the one with Sophia's necklace, he snatched up the cup and grabbed the piece of jewelry along with his coin box, and raced off down the porch steps.

"Hey, come back here you. Momma gave me that," Sophia said, realizing Astuto had been playing her the whole time like a pool hustler. She heard her father call out her name and figured she'd get her necklace back from the sly troll later.

She ran down the porch steps and joined her father, who was leading the brown and white pinto out of its stall. He looped the reins around the fence post.

Sophia reached up and stroked the horse's cheek.

"That's good," Miguel said. "He likes that."

"Am I going to ride Scout?" Sophia asked. She was wearing a cotton shirt, long jean skirt, a pair of cowgirl boots, and one of Camilla's sombreros with a chin string.

"Yeah, he's more your size. Let me show you how to saddle him up. First we start with a fitted pad." Miguel placed the thick, contoured pad onto Scout's back. "Next goes the blanket for added protection." Miguel made sure the heavy fabric was situated evenly on both sides of the horse. He grabbed the Western saddle off the top railing. "Now goes the saddle."

"Is it heavy?" Sophia asked.

"I'm guessing this one weighs about fifty pounds," Miguel replied, swinging the saddle up and lowering it onto the pinto's back. "First we cinch the front, then the back." He reached under the horse's barrel and grabbed the end of the leather strap. He ran the end through the buckle and cinched the belt. "You don't want to make it too tight." He fastened the other strap securing the rear of the saddle. He slipped his fingers under the pad just behind the withers. "Always leave just a little room. Go tell your mom and Abuela we're almost ready to leave."

"Okay," Sophia said and ran to the house.

Miguel went into the stable and brought out the Appaloosa. He was almost done saddling up Poco when Sophia came running back followed by Maria and Camilla. Both women were carrying something: Maria two canteens with leather lanyards and a lunch bag for Miguel and Sophia to take on the trail; Camilla a Winchester lever action carbine in case of trouble.

"Here's some sandwiches and snacks," Maria said, giving Miguel the bag. She walked over to each horse and hung the canteens on the saddle horns.

Camilla handed Miguel a box of .357 cartridges and the rifle. "That'll stop anything that tries to mess with you."

"Well, I hope I won't have to put it to the test." Miguel stood beside Poco and slipped the rifle into the scabbard strapped behind the cantle. He opened the flap on the saddlebag and stuffed in the box of ammunition along with the sack lunch.

Miguel turned to Sophia. "Here, let me help you up." He waited until Sophia had her left foot firmly in the stirrup and hoisted her up into the saddle. He draped the split reins on each side of Scout's neck then handed the ends up to Sophia. "Wrap each rein around your first three fingers and make a fist. If you want Scout to go left, tug on the rein in your left hand, but not too hard or you'll hurt his mouth. The same goes with the right one. If you want to stop, pull back on both reins. Got it?"

Sophia did as instructed. "Got it!"

"Spoken like a true cowgirl," Camilla said, clapping her hands.

"Promise you two will be careful out there," Maria said. She stepped over and patted Sophia's leg.

"We will," Sophia answered.

Maria looked over at Miguel. He gave her a slight shrug and smiled. "We won't go far. Be back before supper."

"Tread softly," Camilla said.

"Always," Miguel replied and climbed into the saddle. He grabbed the reins and steered the Appaloosa through the gate. He looked over his shoulder and saw that Sophia was right behind, riding Scout like a natural.

Maria and Camilla waved as though Miguel and Sophia were setting out on a cattle drive and wouldn't be back for a real long time.

Miguel made Poco sidestep so Sophia could ride up beside him. "How does it feel?" he asked.

"Good," Sophia said with a smile.

"Great. Let's go." He used his boot heel to nudge Poco into a slow trot. Not wanting to be left behind, Scout quickened his stride until both horses were cantering side by side.

Miguel laughed when Sophia—bouncing in the saddle with both hands around the horn—let out a joyous girlish cheer, "Yahoo Scout!"

Worried his daughter could be thrown before they had even set out, Miguel pulled back on the reins. As soon as Poco returned to a walk, so did Scout as the pinto had a bad case of being a buddy sour horse, which meant that Scout suffered separation anxiety whenever he wasn't able to be with Poco. It was good to know that Scout would always follow Poco's lead.

"I was having fun," Sophia protested. "How come they slowed down?"

"You keep bouncing up and down like that you're going to have saddle sores the size of pancakes."

"For real?"

"Oh yeah," Miguel said. "Trust me. I know."

"So where are we going?" Sophia asked.

"To a special place." Miguel could tell by the look on Sophia's face that she was excited to see where her father spent his time when he was her age. It was times like this Miguel cherished the most when he could share moments of his youth where they could relate, knowing this is when he truly connected with his daughter instead of letting their relationship drift apart with her attention consumed by computer games and constantly chatting online with her friends.

Miguel figured coming to Camilla's was going to be a nice little break from all of that and looked forward to a good time bonding with his daughter.

21

WOLF IN LLAMA'S CLOTHING

Roxy parked the Mustang Interceptor by the front entrance of the animal rescue and climbed out of her car. She could hear bleating and baying and the steady barking of dogs coming from behind the building.

She spotted Ben's Tahoe next to a pickup and a deisel truck with a long livestock trailer attached to the rear bumper. The pickup had large wire cages in the bed big enough for transporting not only domestic strays but also smaller neglected farm animals. There was also the local veterinarian's SUV with the clinic's template on the driver's-side door.

She walked down the side of the building to an eight-foot-tall cyclone fence that stretched around a five-acre parcel filled with a hodgepodge of animals common to New Mexico. A few cattle, some horses, mules, and donkeys all feeding off of hay bales that had been dumped randomly from the back of a truck to allow the animals plenty of space.

Small herds of sheep and goats congregated together, all of them rescued from one bad situation or another. Many times farmers and ranchers were unable to care for the animals due to a death of a family member critical in running the operation or a foreclosure on the property and were forced to relinquish their livestock.

Roxy could hear chickens clucking from a large coop. Dogs yelping from kennels that weren't out wandering about.

Besides the normal animals one would expect to see at a rescue, there were also exotic ones as well. She spotted llamas, and their smaller cousins, alpacas, roaming about along with a handful of ostriches. It was definitely a sight to see. She often wondered why different species of animals could coexist without any problem where humans always had trouble getting along.

Roxy spotted a small group of people gathered by the fence a hundred yards away inside the enclosure. She opened the gate, stepped in, and shut the gate behind her. She strode through the field. Every time she came close to an animal it would take one look at her and shy away. She did her best to ignore them and kept on walking.

Finally she was close enough and recognized Ben standing with the rescue's owner, Clay Lansford. They were staring down at the town's veterinarian, Tanya Campbell, crouched over a large furry animal lying on the ground.

"I got here as soon as I could," Roxy said. "What happened?"

"Something attacked my guard llama, Mimi," Clay said.

Roxy watched Tanya inject a needle into the shoulder of the four-hundred-pound llama that was breathing shallowly. Parts of its back and flank had been slashed leaving red ribbons of exposed flesh in its brown fur.

"I saw her take down a wolf once and stomp out its guts," Clay said. "Whatever did this had to be one mean son of a bitch."

"She's lucky the cuts weren't any deeper," Tanya said. "I'd like to get her to the clinic as soon as possible."

"I'll get some of the volunteers to help load her into the back of my truck."

"Great," Tanya said. "I gave her a tranquilizer so she'll be out for a while."

Roxy looked around expecting to see a hole in the fence where the predator might have used to crawl through and attack the llama. She gazed down the fence that bordered a grove of hackberry elms but didn't see any breach where it might have gained entry. "How do you figure it got in?" she asked.

"Don't rightly know," Clay said. "Short of climbing the fence."

"Is it possible someone left a gate open?" Ben asked.

"Maybe but not likely. All of our volunteers are highly trained."

"Want me to scout around?" Roxy asked Ben.

"See if you can spot any tracks. I'll lend a hand here," Ben said.

While the others were preparing to transport the injured llama, Roxy went back the way she had come. She walked along the outside perimeter of the fence line and entered the copse of elms, keeping her eyes on the ground. She glanced over her shoulder and could no longer see the fence that protected the grounds of the animal rescue.

She heard a moan and stopped. The sound was directly ahead. Roxie looked down and saw scuff marks in the dirt.

Again she heard a groan. She couldn't tell if it was human or an animal.

She cupped her palm around the handgrip of her service weapon, ready to draw in a split second if she had to.

Taking a few cautionary steps, she saw a pair of bare feet then the hairy legs of a man partially hidden behind a tree trunk. Roxie took another step and froze. "You stupid shit!" she cursed.

"Sorry. I know, I know," Ethan said, lying naked on the ground and writhing with pain. His chest and the skin around his navel were purple bruises from the pummeling hooves of the guard llama.

Roxie knelt to examine her brother's injuries. "I hate to say it."

"What?" Ethan said, clutching his stomach.

"You'll live. Give it a minute." She couldn't contain her anger any longer and punched Ethan in the shoulder.

"Hey! I'm in enough pain."

"What were you thinking?" Roxie said. "You know better than to hunt so close to home."

"I couldn't wait."

"You better get out of here," Roxie said.

"Or what? You'll call the cops," Ethan replied, obviously feeling better, the pain slowly dissipating.

"Not funny. Go, before Ben sees you."

Ethan got to his feet, the healing process already taking effect and changing the coloring of the bruises to yellow. Soon they would be gone altogether. He looked at Roxie with that same apologetic look she had seen so many times before.

"You heard me, get out of here!" Roxie said sternly.

Ethan took a couple of steps back, turned swiftly, and loped off between the trees.

Roxie shook her head. She had warned him, time and time again, especially when they were kids growing up, but Ethan never seemed to get it. No matter how hard she tried to knock sense into him. Sooner or later, Ethan was going to get caught. And that wouldn't be good for her or her other brother, Kane. If Kane were to find out Ethan had played this little stunt at the animal rescue, all hell would break loose.

As always it was up to her to keep the peace.

Which was the main reason she'd taken the job of deputy in the first place.

22

BOX CANYON

Every time Felix paid her a visit to pick up her latest artwork, Vera always rewarded herself with a tall glass of wine. So after he left, she did just that, even though she knew she had an hour-long drive ahead of her. She'd gathered up the blank canvas with the easel and her paint supplies and took them out to the Jeep truck, placing them on the rear seat. Even though she had a bit of a buzz from the wine, she had a clear enough mind to make sure she brought along her cell phone and plenty of bottled water.

But when she was more than halfway to her destination she realized she had forgotten to bring along her camera, which wasn't a complete disaster as she had planned to paint her real-life subject on location, praying that the lechugilla hadn't already blossomed and died.

What she hadn't planned was finding an apparent landslide blocking the entrance to the box canyon where the lechugilla had been growing for the past quarter of a century.

"Damn." She stopped the Jeep and surveyed the rubble blocking her path. The boulders were piled six feet high and were covered with loose rock and shale. There was a spot she thought she might be able to navigate over onto the other side without any problem.

Vera edged the four-wheel Jeep forward. The ground sloped slightly and the front all-terrain tires gripped the rock like cat claws. Vera held the steering wheel steady while the truck muscled its way up onto the flat top of a boulder.

"Come on, baby, you can do it." She felt the adrenaline rush and knew Ben would be impressed knowing she wasn't going to be deterred by a silly rockslide.

But then on the way down the rocks shifted and the Jeep's chassis came crashing down, the jolt jarring her back. Her hands slipped off the steering wheel. The Jeep slid sideways off the rock and came to a halt.

Vera opened her door. She scooted off the seat onto the ground, grabbing the small of her back with her right hand. "Jesus that hurt!" She stepped away from the vehicle and walked around, hoping to ease the pain. Even though her back was sore, she was certain she hadn't sustained any permanent damage to her spine.

From where she stood, she could see the lone lechugilla in the pocket of the box canyon. In its final day it stood 16 feet tall and was in full bloom, the seedpods gaping like serpent heads.

Time was of the essence.

She shook off the pain and opened the rear door. She grabbed the canvas and easel and walked a hundred yards where she set up a few feet away from the plant.

On her way back to collect her paint supplies, she noticed something black pooled under the Jeep. She got down on her hands and knees and looked under the vehicle.

A rock had punched a hole in the pan and oil was leaking out onto the sand.

"Shit!" She fished her cell phone out of her jean pocket. She went to call Ben then realized she wasn't getting a signal. "Come on, now what?" She knew if she wanted to get a clear signal she would have to get out of the canyon but that would mean losing her chance to paint the quickly demising plant while it was still in bloom.

She had only a couple of hours of sunlight.

It was now or never.

Vera grabbed her paint supplies and rushed back to her easel.

23

THE HOGAN

"What is it?" Sophia asked, riding alongside her father as they approached the weathered structure that looked as though it had been there for centuries. Timber rafters protruded from the base of the dome roof comprised of dry mud and thatch. The small building had an igloo design but instead of blocks of ice, the circular shape was made up of a cinder block pattern of red adobe clay, a rectangular entrance with no door and two square windows void of glass.

"It's an old Navajo dwelling. They call it a hogan."

"Does anyone live there?" Sophia asked.

"I doubt anyone's lived there in years." Miguel reined in Poco. He grabbed the horn and swung his leg over the cantle, stepping down off the stirrups. He walked the Appaloosa to the shady side of the hogan where there was a small patch of prairie grass and the horse would be out of the sun. He tied the reins around the bough of a dead mesquite tree.

Before he could help Sophia down from her horse, Scout was already ambling over to be with Poco. Miguel assisted Sophia in climbing down from the saddle. He tethered Scout alongside Poco. Both horses were content to graze.

Grabbing the lunch sack from the saddlebag, Miguel unhooked both canteens. He had no idea what the outdoor temperature was at the moment as it was a dry heat but he figured it had to be in the high nineties. He decided to bring the Winchester carbine and pulled it out of the scabbard. "Let's go inside. It'll be much cooler."

They walked over to the dark entrance. "Let me check before we go in," Miguel said. "Make sure there aren't any pesky critters."

Rays of sunshine filtered inside the single-room abode. A small wooden table was in the center with two rickety chairs.

Miguel went in and placed the canteens and lunch sack on a chair then leaned the rifle against the wall. He spotted a tumbleweed that had blown in. He grabbed the dried-up ball of dead bush and dragged it along the dirt, checking for anything that might be hiding underneath. There was nothing but dusty soil.

"It's safe to come in," he said.

Sophia stepped onto the threshold and glanced inside.

"Let's sit at the table," Miguel said, "and see what they packed for us."

Miguel waited for Sophia to occupy the empty chair then wiped the dust off the table with his shirtsleeve, took the two canteens and the sack lunch, and put them on the tabletop. He opened the lunch sack and handed Sophia a sandwich wrapped in wax paper along with her canteen. He took out his own sandwich and saw that the women had also packed a baggy of jerky and some dried apricots.

Miguel peeked between the two thick slices of home baked bread and saw a generous layer of apricot jam. He closed the sandwich and took a big bite. He looked over at Sophia who was munching away. Apricots were her favorite.

In between mouthfuls, Miguel said, "The Indians always built their dwellings facing east."

"Why's that?" Sophia asked, wiping a dapple of jam from her lower lip.

"That way they could always look out and see the sun rise every morning."

"So, is this place special?" Sophia took a drink from her canteen.

"It is," Miguel said with a grin. "Abuela brought me here once when I was a kid. I thought it was pretty cool. I always imagined what it might have been like living back then."

Miguel collected the wrappings and stuffed them in the lunch sack. "There's something I want you to see, if it's still here." He got up from the table. He stepped over to the concave wall where there was a narrow shelf tucked between two clay cinder blocks. He reached in and took out a small metal box. Miguel brought the tin over to the table and sat down.

"What's in it?" Sophia asked.

Miguel opened the lid and gingerly tipped the contents onto the rough surface of the table. "Take a look."

Sophia gazed at the artifacts. She studied the etching on a copper bracelet.

"Like it?" Miguel asked.

"I love it."

"Check out the other stuff."

Sophia ran her fingers along a turquoise beaded necklace then weighed a rough-cut jade stone in the palm of her hand. There were half a dozen silver rings. Two fit her small fingers perfectly but she removed them and put them back in the tin. Next was a beat-up pack of Bicycle playing cards along with a few cartridge shells from different caliber guns.

Miguel put a casing up to his lips and blew, making a whistling noise.

"Let me try." Sophia picked up a brass casing and was able to duplicate the same sound.

"You should start a band."

"Yeah, right." She reached down and picked up a silver coin. "What's this?"

"Looks like a silver dollar. Minted back in the 1800s. Might be worth something."

"You think so?"

"Never know." Miguel watched as Sophia carefully gathered everything up and put it back in the tin. "You don't want any of it?" he asked.

"It's not mine."

"True," Miguel said, feeling a rush of pride knowing that he and Maria had taught their daughter well. "Maybe someone will come and reclaim it one day."

"I hope so," Sophia said.

Poco and Scout let out fearful cries and began stomping the ground.

"What's wrong with them?" Sophia asked.

"I don't know, something's got them spooked." Miguel grabbed the rifle. He and Sophia went outside and dashed around back to where the horses were tied up.

A diamondback was coiled at the base of the old mesquite tree, shaking its rattler.

Poco and Scout reared up on their hind legs, kicking their front hooves, frantically trying to get away from the menacing snake ready to strike.

Before Miguel could take aim, Poco snapped his reins tied to the bough. Scout was so scared, he almost tripped and fell, and then he too broke free. Both horses took off in a hard gallop and raced away into the desert.

"Stupid horses," Miguel said.

"Where are they going?" Sophia asked.

"Back to the barn."

"How are we going to get back?"

"How do you think?"

"You mean *walk*? For how far?" Sophia asked.

"I think we covered about ten miles," Miguel said, knowing that when the horses got back to the barn his mother and Maria would be frantic worrying what had happened.

"But won't Mom and Abuela come looking for us?"

"I would hope so, but there's a slight problem."

"What's that?"

"I never told them where we were going," Miguel confessed, feeling the fool for jeopardizing his daughter's safety and getting them stranded in the desert.

"Oh my God, the snake," Sophia gasped.

Miguel glanced over at the mesquite tree. The rattler was gone. "Must have slithered back into its hole."

Then he thought to check the rifle to see if it was loaded. He ratcheted the lever. A bullet ejected out the top of the chamber and fell to the dirt. He continued until there were six bullets on the ground by his feet. He picked them up, blew off any grit, and inserted them back into the side feed. "Good thing Abuela thought to load the gun or we would be defenseless as Poco ran off with the box of ammunition."

"So what are we going to do?"

"Well, I think we should wait for it to cool down. Then we'll go."

"In the dark? Won't we get lost?" Sophia asked.

"Don't worry. Tonight should be a clear sky with a full moon. I'll teach you how to read the stars. Think you're up for it? It'll take us maybe three hours."

"I can do it," Sophia said bravely.

"Good girl." Miguel was proud of her and patted Sophia on the shoulder. "Come back inside and we can play some cards."

"Can we play kings in the corner?"

"You bet."

24

WHO'S THERE

Macy's shift was going to be up soon. She was beat. Everything that could go wrong seemed to be doing just that. The drawer on the cash register kept sticking and giving her problems each time she wanted to put money in the till and hand out change to the customers. If that wasn't annoying enough, the slushy machine wasn't working.

Then someone had dropped a six-pack of bottled beer on the floor in the back sending suds and shattered glass everywhere. By the time she grabbed a mop and bucket to clean it up, the bungling thief had snuck down the aisle and ran out the door but not before snatching the donation jar for wayward children off the counter.

Often times she felt more like a security guard than a gas station convenience store clerk having to always keep a vigilant eye on everyone that came in, especially the teenagers with their *sticky fingers*. Even though she was supposed to avoid confrontation if she witnessed a potential pilfering in progress, she ignored the rules and laid into the thieves, threatening them with bodily harm if they didn't put whatever it was they were about to steal back on the shelf and get the hell out of her store.

She wondered if the boys would be home when she got off and what she might cook for dinner if they were. Lately, they had been choosing to spend time at their friends' houses and eating there, rather than with her. She knew they were probably drinking and doing drugs but when she asked them about it, they always denied that they were and it had become a big problem, eroding their relationship.

Ethan had been the perfect sounding board for trying to get into her kids' minds as he confessed to having recently kicked a serious drug habit though he still smoked weed.

But now, she wasn't so sure being with Ethan was such a good idea, especially after she saw his violent side last night. The way he had viciously lashed out at that biker even though the man had it coming and then that strange noise she heard Ethan make when he was behind the table.

And why had Kane rushed Ethan out of the bar?

The chime sounded and the glass door automatically opened.

Macy went behind the counter and walked up to the register, missing whoever it was that had just come into the store as they had disappeared down one of the aisles. She looked up at the round mirror mounted near the ceiling on the far side of the store but she couldn't see anyone, which gave her pause. She hoped they weren't carrying.

It always made her uncomfortable whenever someone came into the store with a visible weapon. She knew she couldn't deny them access to the store, as it was legal to carry a firearm as long as the person had a permit. She often wondered what would stop them from robbing her at gunpoint. Or if they tried a *five-finger discount* if they would even give her a second thought and just walk out with their free merchandise knowing she would be less inclined to tangle with someone armed.

She kept looking at the large mirror, hoping to spot the person, but whoever it was, was doing a good job of not being seen.

"Can I help you?" Macy called out.

She got no reply.

Macy looked out the front window of the store. The parking lot was empty.

Which meant whoever was in the store had parked on the side of the building so as not to be seen by the outside security cameras. Something the Quick Stop Killer would do, as the police still didn't have a description of his car.

Macy touched the baseball bat behind the counter, wishing it were a double barrel shotgun instead.

Even though the store was air-conditioned, sweat drizzled down between her shoulder blades to the small of her back.

She glanced at her cell phone on the counter. Sheriff Lobo was number 4 on speed dial if need be.

A glass jar shattered on the floor.

"Hey, what are you doing back there?" she yelled. "You better not be breaking stuff!" Even though she was nervous as hell and feared for her life, she would be damned if she was going to let some creep come in and wreck the store.

She heard a strange sound on the other side of the aisle like wood cracking under pressure.

Macy grabbed the baseball bat. "You need to leave!"

She could hear raspy breathing as she came out from behind the counter. She grabbed her cell phone, scrolled through her contacts, and punched in the number for the sheriff. Macy put the phone up to her ear, hoping someone would pick up, but it went directly to voicemail. "Shit," she said.

Macy walked over to the end of the shelf, raised the bat over her shoulder ready to swing, and stepped into the aisle.

There was no one there, just a broken jar of pickles on the floor.

She could smell rank breath, feel the hotness of it on the back of her neck. She turned slightly and came face to face with a monstrous creature with glaring black eyes and vicious fangs.

Hot blades of fire sliced through her abdomen.

She looked down and saw the front of her blue smock shredded and her insides spilling out of a large gash across her stomach. She cocked her head to gaze up at her attacker but then her legs gave out and she fell to the floor.

Lying on her side in a growing pool of blood she watched the thing run out of the store.

Her cell phone began ringing.

About time, Sheriff! A little late don't you think?

The persistent ring tone soon stopped.

And that is when Macy's eyes drooped closed.

25

BARN-SPOILED

Maria was sweeping the porch when she heard the horses gallop up and trot inside the barn. She opened the screen door and hollered, "Camilla, they're back!"

Camilla stepped out the door, removed her apron, and tossed it on the rocking chair. "Let's go help them with the horses." They walked over to the barn entrance and stepped inside.

Poco and Scout were in their respective stalls, still wearing their saddles.

Maria glanced around. "Where are Miguel and Sophia?"

Camilla approached Poco. The Appaloosa was skittish and stepped back when Camilla tried to touch it.

"My Lord, they're lathered up." White shaving cream like foam covered each horse's chest and legs. "They must have run full gallop all the way back. It's a wonder they didn't collapse from heat exhaustion."

"You don't think Miguel and Sophia got bucked off, do you?" Maria asked.

"Not Miguel. He's a good rider. I don't think Miguel and Sophia were on them at the time. That's what happens when you got a couple of barn-spoiled horses. First chance they get, they're leaving you high and dry and running back to the barn."

"We have to go look for them," Maria said in a panic.

"We will. But first we need to tend to the animals."

Maria helped Camilla unsaddle the horses and wipe them down with wet sponges.

Inside the house, Camilla went into her room to gather up some things to take along while Maria dashed into the guest room for the truck keys. She came out and joined Camilla in the kitchen. "Any idea where they might have gone?"

"Maybe," Camilla said.

"Where's that?" Maria asked, grabbing two canteens hanging on the wall and filling one with cold water from the tap on the kitchen sink.

"An abandoned Navaho hogan I once took Miguel to. Better grab some flashlights out of the drawer."

"Okay," Maria said. She finished filling the second canteen and retrieved the flashlights. She turned around and saw Camilla holding a shotgun. "That wouldn't by any chance be the same gun you talked about in your story?"

"Sure is. Grainger's Ithaca 10-guage," Camilla said, opening the breech on the 12-inch double barrel coach gun to make sure it was loaded then snapping it shut.

"So everything you told us *was* true?" Maria said.

"Most of it," Camilla said.

Maria leaned forward and stared down at the table.

"Are you okay?" Camilla asked.

"I just need a second," Maria answered but didn't look up.

"Don't worry, we'll find them. Do you have something of Sophia's?"

"Sure." Maria went into the guest bedroom and came out with one of her daughter's shirts.

Camilla turned and yelled, "Astuto! Get in here! Now!"

They waited but the little troll didn't respond.

"Astuto! You better get in here! We have to find Sophia!"

This time the little-wrinkly-old-man-looking troll came out of his hole in the wall and scampered over to Camilla's feet.

Camilla leaned down and showed Astuto Sophia's shirt. "Now I want you to take a good whiff."

Astuto buried his face into the fabric and snorted.

"Good grief, did he just blow his nose?" Maria said. "You really think he can find them?"

"You bet. Astuto's got a nose like a bloodhound."

26

CLEAN UP ON AISLE ONE

After assisting Clay Lansford with his injured llama, Ben had waited by his Tahoe for Roxy to return from her search. As soon as he saw her come out of the trees, a car engine sounded off in the distance. "Anything?" he asked.

"No," Roxy replied.

The sun had dipped behind the treetops casting long shadows across the menagerie of animals scattered about the field.

"You want to write this one up?" Ben said to Roxy.

"Not much to write up."

"Yeah, you can do it in the morning. I have to stop by the Quick Stop and pick up a few things on the way home."

"I'll follow you. The Interceptor needs filling up."

"Damn gas guzzler's putting a crimp in my budget," Ben griped. "If I'd known, I'd have put in for a hybrid."

"Sure, I can see myself telling speeders 'You mind pulling over while I recharge my battery,'" Roxie quipped. "Besides, I like that car."

"I can tell. Let's go." Ben climbed into his Tahoe while Roxy got in the Mustang.

The trip over to the Quick Stop took only fifteen minutes.

Ben parked in front of the convenience store entrance. He got out and saw Roxy pull up to the nearest gas pump. She exited the Mustang, grabbed the nozzle off the pump, and began gassing up her vehicle.

Entering the store, Ben knew something was wrong when he saw no one at the counter and the place had a strange odor. It smelled like rancid food that had been left out in the sun to spoil. He could hear the drone of buzzing flies. The sound was coming from the other side of the far end of the aisle. "Macy, you in here?" he hollered.

He waited for a reply, but none came. He glanced out the glass doors. Roxy had finished filling the car and was returning the nozzle to the pump. She began walking toward the front entrance.

When the automatic glass doors opened, Ben waved to her and called out, "We might have a problem." He drew his gun from the holster slowly.

Roxy pulled out her service weapon, held it with both hands, and advanced toward Ben. "What is—my God, what's that smell?"

"I don't know," Ben replied.

Roxy glanced around. "Where's Macy? Isn't she supposed to be working today?"

Ben edged around the end of the first row of shelves. He looked down the aisle and gasped, "Oh no." He hurried down but could only go so far or he would be stepping in blood.

There was so much blood.

He remembered Monroe telling him that a human body weighing 150 pounds contained just over a gallon of blood; which when put in perspective was enough to paint half a small bedroom.

Or pool a huge section of floor.

"Oh my God, it's Macy," Roxy said.

"Go down the other aisle and check the back," Ben instructed Roxie. He waited while she went to the rear room.

"All clear. There's no one here," she yelled.

"Call Monroe and Forensics."

"Will do." Roxie came back and went out to her car.

Ben tried to get as close as he could without disturbing the evidence. Macy's midsection looked like she had fallen on the spinning blade of a buzz saw. It was a terrible sight. What was he going to tell her boys?

He took a step back and glanced over the top shelf.

Roxie stood outside next to her patrol car. Instead of using her radio inside the cruiser, she was talking on her cell phone, which he didn't think was unusual.

It was the way she was acting that struck him as odd.

Even though he couldn't hear what she was saying, he could tell she was yelling at the person on the other end of the line. Ben doubted very seriously if it was the coroner or the criminal investigators.

Whoever it was, it was personal, and Roxie was reaming the person good.

27

HEATED CONVERSATION

Roxie had been furious with Ethan over the phone. She'd asked where he had gone after his little stunt at the animal rescue. He swore he had gone straight home to the apartment, but she was skeptical, knowing that after a therianthropic episode it was common for him to experience a temporary fugue. She decided not to press him any further and confront him in person about Macy's death.

She ended her call with Ethan, spotting Ben staring at her through the convenience store window and hoped she hadn't made too much of a spectacle of herself. She immediately contacted Keith Monroe and then afterward called the U.S. Forensic Office to have an investigative team sent out.

Roxie took a deep calming breath, stuffed her cell phone into her trouser pocket, and walked back to the convenience store. "They're on their way," she called out, walking between the automatic doors as they slid open.

"Good," Ben said, standing on the outer perimeter of blood haloed around Macy Brown's body. "You okay?" he asked.

"Yeah, why?"

"Couldn't help noticing you outside. You looked a little agitated. Monroe giving you a hard time?"

"No, nothing like that." Roxie walked over and joined Ben. They both gazed down at the bloody corpse.

"What kind of monster could do something like this?" Ben said.

"Think it was the Quick Stop Killer?"

"I checked the register. Doesn't look like anyone touched the money. This is definitely an animal attack. Probably the same thing that killed the Willards." Ben turned and looked at the front entrance. "I'll bet anything it waltzed right through those doors and when Macy tried to run, the damn thing chased her down and killed her."

28

MOONLIGHT PREDATORS

Miguel stepped out of the hogan and gazed up at the night sky. Just as he had predicted there was a full moon with no clouds and plenty of stars to help them navigate back to Camilla's house. "Ready to go?" he asked Sophia.

"So how do you know which way?" she asked.

"Easy. Look up." Miguel pointed. "See those three stars aligned together?"

Sophia stared for a moment, then said, "Yes."

"That's Orion's belt. It's pointing east, which is the way back to Abuela's."

"You mean it's that simple?"

"Not everything has to be complicated. Come on." Miguel rested the carbine on his shoulder and took Sophia's hand. Even though the temperature hadn't dropped by much and was still warm, they didn't have to contend with the scorching sun.

Walking through the desert, Miguel began their lesson. He pointed at the stars that represented Orion's sword hanging off the belt and that the bottom star indicated due south and in another constellation the brightest star was Polaris or commonly called the North Star.

They hadn't gone more than half a mile when Sophia squeezed her father's hand and said quietly, "Papa, I heard something."

"I did too. To your left?"

"Yes."

He had heard them earlier but didn't want to alarm Sophia. It was difficult to estimate how many there were but he figured it was a small pack of around six, maybe more. He wasn't sure if they would try to attack. Generally they were cowardly but if there were enough of them, they might be emboldened being in a large group.

He heard movement to his right, the sound of taloned feet scrambling behind a stand of tarbush, which meant the nocturne predators were stalking them on both sides.

Miguel lifted the gun barrel off his shoulder and held the rifle at his side. He would need two hands to shoot it properly but at the moment the last thing he wanted to do was let go of Sophia's hand.

“Papa, I’m scared.” Sophia rushed forward, almost pulling her hand out of Miguel’s grip.

“No, we can’t run. We do and they’ll be on us in a flash.”

An eerie screech pierced the desert calm.

“What are they?” Sophia asked, cocking her head to see what it was.

“I think they’re chupacabras.”

“How do you know?”

“I’ve seen their tracks.” Miguel heard something scamper to his right and gazed out at the silhouettes in the night. It was difficult to tell if they were vegetation or creatures poised to strike. And then one bolted out from behind a bush.

The chupacabra was hunched, four feet tall, and raced across the sand on two hind legs. It had fish eyes, an egg-shaped head, and needle-tipped teeth in a bowl-shaped mouth. Bony knobs grew out of its spiny back down to its serpentine tail. It had claws like a dog on its front legs and bird-like talons on its rear feet.

The creature screeched, sounding like the one they had heard previously and charged Miguel and Sophia. Miguel let go of Sophia’s hand, aimed the Winchester at the hideous thing, and fired.

The bullet punched through the chupacabra’s forehead and blew out the back of its skull. It kept running for a few more steps then crashed to the ground. Miguel cocked the lever action, spitting out the empty shell and rammed a new cartridge into the chamber.

Another bloodsucker darted out of the darkness. It was faster and dodged Miguel’s next shot. Miguel put another round in the chamber and fired. This time the bullet kneecapped the creature and blew off its leg. It stumbled and fell in front of Miguel. He levered another bullet into the chamber, pointed the muzzle down, and finished off the chupacabra with a single shot, its head shattering like a crystal bowl knocked off a shelf.

Sophia screamed.

Miguel spun around and saw his daughter dragged away into the dark.

29

BOXED IN

Vera knew time was of the essence. With only a narrow window of sunlight left, she had worked as fast as she could, dabbing in the backdrop outline around the outer edges, leaving enough blank canvas to sketch in her subject. But then as the sun began to set, the lighting kept changing and creating shadows, making it near impossible to capture the exact moment; which she could have accomplished if she had used a photograph of the lechugilla for her template.

As nightfall approached she finalized her last brush stroke. Even in the dim light she could tell it was one of her better works, if not the best. Gene would definitely be impressed and would no doubt get top dollar at the gallery and a well-earned commission.

She had made two trips back to the Jeep; the first one carrying the finished painting. Opening the rear passenger door, she placed the canvas on the floor, resting it against the front of the backseat. She collected her easel and paint supplies, and put them in the cab. She thought about trying to start the Jeep but knew it would only ruin the engine if she tried driving it with no oil as most of it had spilled out onto the ground from the ruptured pan.

Her only choice would be to call Ben. Tell him where she was and have him come out and get her. She took her cell phone out of her pocket and pressed his contact number but the call wouldn't go through as the screen showed no signal. The only way to get hold of Ben was to walk out of the box canyon and maybe find some high ground. The thought of being stranded overnight in the desert frightened her.

Vera grabbed a flashlight out of the glove compartment. She tested it to make sure it worked and began climbing up the pile of rocks blocking the mouth of the canyon.

Reaching the top, she heard small boulders cascading down the cliff face. She got down and covered her head with her hands. Aggregate and heavy stones rained down all around her, some bouncing and striking the back of the Jeep.

Once she was sure the minor avalanche had stopped, she continued down to the base of the rock pile.

She looked at her cell phone screen—still no signal.

"Oh, come on." Vera took a deep breath to settle her nerves. She knew she was completely helpless, as no one knew where she was. It was ironic to think that her last painting was of death and she would be dying along with it.

Something big swooped down over her head.

Sharp talons scraped along her scalp and tore out some of her hair. "Jesus, what the hell?" she swore. Vera looked up but whatever had ambushed her had flown into the shadows. She touched the top of her head and felt a warm stickiness.

She was a sitting duck out in the open and needed to get back to the Jeep.

Staying as low as possible, Vera scrambled back up the rock pile. She could hear the sound of powerful wings coming her way. She flattened on the rocks just as the thing passed over, its razor-sharp claws ripping the back of her shirt.

What the hell is it?

It's too big to be a bat or even a hawk.

Vera didn't wait around to find out.

Coming down the opposite side of the rocks, she grabbed the first door handle on the Jeep and opened the door.

The dome light came on, illuminating the cab.

Vera was struck in the shoulder and slammed into the side of the Jeep, striking her head on the driver's window.

Dazed, Vera caught a glimpse of the thing grabbing the canvas out of the Jeep with its talon feet like a cat roughhousing with a toy.

"No, no!" she screamed, waving her fist at the creature as it flew off with her painting. "You son of a bitch!"

Vera slammed the passenger door and got in behind the steering wheel, shutting the door behind her, which automatically turned off the dome light. Sitting in the dark, the only thing she could think of was all of her planning and hard work down the drain.

"Damn," she cursed and slapped the steering wheel.

A loud thud rattled the hood.

Vera pointed her flashlight at the windshield and turned it on.

The thing was as big as a medium-sized dog, greenish in color, with a large head with two bulging white eyes, a flat snout, and a huge mouth with menacing sharp teeth and an extremely long tongue. It had two short wings and long legs with three-talon feet and was standing on its tiptoes like a bizarre ballerina.

It glared at Vera and lurched, thinking it could bite her but only ended up gnashing its teeth on the hard surface of the glass. It tried again, this time cracking the windshield and leaving a blob of wet drool laced with splats of blood.

The winged chupacabra screeched and flew off.

Vera pushed the Start button on the ignition, lowered her window an inch, and listened while more of them circled above the Jeep.

30

THE SCENT-HOUND

Astuto had been quick to pick up Sophia's scent. Even though Maria could see adequately in the dark with the high beams and the desert floor was relatively flat without too many obstructions, she maintained a speed of no more than fifteen miles per hour for fear she might run over the short troll running in front of the truck if she went any faster.

Maria leaned over the steering wheel, never letting Astuto out of her sight. He had a tendency to zigzag left and right like an evasive deer being pursued, which was maddening because Maria thought she had to follow his exact path.

"Just keep driving straight," Camilla said from the other side of the cab, "before you get us both carsick."

"What's he carrying?" Maria asked, noticing Astuto was holding something in his right hand.

"It's a flint knife," Camilla said. "He carved it out of obsidian. He's quite the craftsman."

"Seriously, he made that?"

"There's a lot that tiny brain of his can do."

Maria cut the wheel to avoid a small boulder. The right tire clipped the rock and the front end rose up a few inches then slammed back down. "Sorry about that," Maria apologized.

"That's all right," Camilla said. "Just watch you don't squish Astuto."

The troll stopped dead in his tracks directly in front of the truck causing Maria to stomp on the brakes. The hood loomed over the small figure. "Oh no! Tell me, tell me I didn't..."

Astuto scampered back into the light, following the trail into the desert.

"Thank God," Maria gasped.

"Drive, drive or we'll lose him," Camilla said, waving her hand.

Maria tromped on the accelerator.

They soon saw Astuto but this time he wasn't alone. He was confronting four hideous creatures twice his size huddled around a person on the ground.

"Oh my God," Maria screamed. "It's Sophia!" Maria knew the creatures were chupacabras from pictures she had seen in one of Miguel's cryptid journals. They were the creepiest things she had ever seen.

"Stay with the truck," Camilla said, throwing open her door. She hopped out with the 10-guage shotgun.

Astuto waved his knife back and forth to scare away the chupacabras.

A creature lunged at the troll.

Astuto leaped in the air, grabbing the chupacabra by the shoulder, and swung himself onto its back. Like a warrior in the heat of battle, the troll stabbed the creature repeatedly in the neck with a series of quick jabs, riding the dying bloodsucker all the way to the ground.

Camilla strode up to a chupacabra and fired both barrels. The thing exploded like a piñata blown to pieces by an M-80.

Two chupacabras hovered over Sophia.

Maria screamed at the creatures. She slammed the horn with the heel of her hand and gunned the engine until it roared like a ferocious beast.

* * *

Miguel saw the approaching headlights. He heard Sophia shouting in the dark as the chattering chupacabras dragged her through the brush.

He ran, stumbling over rocks buried in the sand, but stayed on his feet. He knew he had only two rounds left in the Winchester so he needed to make each shot count.

He could see a small crowd of creatures in the beam of light, circling around something on the ground—Sophia.

Miguel brought the rifle up to shoot but decided against firing as he was afraid he might hit his daughter. The approaching vehicle sounded familiar. He glanced over and saw that it was his truck. Maria and Camilla had found them.

A creature screeched. Miguel watched a small figure riding on a chupacabra's back like a tiny bull rider and stabbing the hell out of it. "Good job, Astuto," he shouted.

Miguel heard a loud blast and saw Camilla standing with the short barrel shotgun.

That's when the truck's horn blared and the engine revved.

Miguel dashed across the sand. He fired into the air hoping it would be enough to scare away the creatures. Most of them took off running but a few stood their ground.

Another loud blast and a chupacabra was cut in half by Camilla's scattergun. She ran over to where Astuto was standing over Sophia, waving his knife like a tiny swashbuckler fighting back a bunch of scallywag pirates.

With only one bullet left, Miguel levered it into the chamber. He picked the closest chupacabra and shot it squarely in the chest. The barrel was still hot but he grabbed it anyway and used the rifle as a club to beat a chupacabra over the head until it could no longer stand.

Camilla got Sophia to her feet.

Miguel swung the Winchester as more creatures appeared and the rifle slipped out of his hands. He turned and ran for the truck.

The cab light was on, the passenger door open.

"Hurry, get inside!" Miguel shouted to Camilla and Sophia.

A chupacabra leaped inside the truck's cab.

Maria turned and put her hands up to fend off the snarling creature, its teeth gnashing at her fingers. She screamed and reached back with her left hand, fumbling for the door handle. The vicious bloodsucker slammed her head against the side window.

"No!" Miguel yelled, racing toward the open door. He reached in, grabbed the chupacabra by a hind foot, and yanked the thing out of the truck. As soon as it hit the ground, Miguel raised his boot and stomped down on its ugly face, killing it instantly.

He scrambled inside the cab.

Maria stared up at the headliner, her eyes vacant; the back of her head resting on the spider-webbed glass splattered with her blood.

31

MAD RUSH

Miguel drove like a mad man; Maria slumped against Camilla pressed against the passenger door, Sophia sobbing in the back seat. The truck bounced over the rough terrain, mowing down cacti, and flattening brush. He knew if he wasn't careful he would drive them straight into a ravine but he was desperate to get Maria to the emergency clinic.

"How far is it to the main road?" Miguel asked his mother.

"Maybe five, six miles," Camilla answered, holding on as they were jostled about in the cab.

"How's she doing?"

Camilla leaned over so she could see Maria's face. "Still unconscious."

"But she's breathing, right?" Miguel said in a panic.

"Papa, is Momma going to die?" Sophia asked, tears running down her cheeks.

Miguel had been so consumed with his driving he had completely forgotten about his daughter. "No, Sophia!" Miguel shouted, and then felt bad for yelling at her. "She is not going to die. Momma will be fine." He shot a glance over at his mother but he could tell by her expression she was skeptical.

Something hit the back window. Miguel glanced in the rearview mirror and saw Astuto flailing about in the truck bed. He looked like a drunken sailor stumbling on a ship's deck in a rough sea. The truck took a hard bump and nearly threw the troll out of the truck.

"Miguel, look out!" Camilla screamed.

Miguel gazed back at the windshield and saw an outcrop of rock straight ahead. He slammed on the brakes, cutting the wheel but it was too late. The front end catapulted over the raised bedrock and the truck soared in the air.

"Hold on!" Miguel yelled.

The vehicle came down, landing bumper first, the right front tire bursting on the sharp rock.

Miguel looked over his shoulder. "Sophia, are you hurt?"

"No, Poppa. I had my seatbelt on."

"Good girl." Miguel turned to his mother.

"We're okay." Camilla said, her left arm tightly wrapped around Maria.

They heard frantic pounding on the back window. Astuto was hitting the glass with his tiny fists and yelling obscenities that only he understood.

"Quiet!" Camilla shouted. The troll hung his head, stalked off to the back of the truck, and jumped out.

Miguel drove on for a short distance but it was obvious they weren't going to get much further with a flat tire. "We must be close to the house," he said.

"It's not far," Camilla said.

Miguel climbed out of the truck. Camilla scooted Maria across the seat and Miguel scooped her up in his arms. Camilla got out on the passenger side and helped Sophia out of the cab.

Taking the lead, Camilla held the flashlight in one hand, Sophia's hand in the other while Miguel followed behind carrying Maria.

"How far is the medical clinic from your house?" Miguel asked. He could see the blood from Maria's head wound on his upper sleeve.

"About ten miles once you get to the main road," Camilla answered.

"Does your phone work because I was having trouble getting a signal?"

"No."

"Then I hope you got gas in your truck," Miguel said.

Camilla stopped, and turned to her son. "Miguel that truck hasn't run in over a year."

"Then how the *hell* are we going to get Maria to this medical clinic?" Miguel snapped.

"I don't know."

32

TELLTALE IMAGE

After Monroe had collected Macy's body from the convenience store and Ben had spent an hour talking with the criminologists, Ben decided to run home before following up at the Coroner's Office. Already dark, Ben anticipated a long evening.

When he walked in the front door, he called out, "Vera! I'm home!" He strolled through the living room and into the kitchen thinking she might be in there. He went straight for the fridge and grabbed a bottled water. Chugging it half down, he put the plastic bottle on the counter, and went down the hall to the bedroom. He stood at the threshold and gazed about the room but Vera was nowhere to be seen.

He went back through the house and opened the door leading into the two-car garage. Vera's Jeep was gone. "Where did you get off to?" he muttered to himself. She hadn't mentioned having to go out. He knew she traveled once a month up to Albuquerque but that wasn't for another two weeks.

Or was it?

He couldn't remember.

Even so, she always left a note as half the time Ben was so distracted with his own work that he often had a memory lapse when it came to keeping track of his wife's often busy schedule. He went into the kitchen and checked the small writing table by the sliding glass doors where she usually left notes for him.

The writing surface was bare except for a blank notepad and a pen.

He went into her studio. As soon as he walked into the room, he noticed that none of the easels had canvases, which meant that Felix had come earlier and packed them up.

Ben was about to leave the room when he noticed Vera's camera on the table. He thought it unusual because she never left the house without it. She always told him that she never knew when she might see something breathtaking that needed to be captured on film so she could later transfer it onto a canvas.

He had an uneasy feeling. He took out his cell phone and tried to give her a call knowing she would see the caller ID and answer. Normally she would pick up on the second or third ring but instead he got her voicemail. He tried again and got no response.

He stepped over to the table and picked up the camera. It was a digital Canon with a long photo lens and a viewing screen on the back face. He turned on the camera and scrolled through the images, recognizing most of the terrain.

Near the end were pictures of the same plant, a tall lechugilla cactus, taken from various angles. Ben didn't remember seeing a painting of it in Vera's studio, which meant she hadn't started it yet, and might explain where she might be.

He brought the camera into his office. Standing by his desk, he scrolled through the images until he found a photo of the mouth of a box canyon taken before the pictures of the lechugilla.

Ben gazed at the large topography map of the Chihuahua Desert hanging on the wall next to his framed achievement awards and diplomas. He traced his finger along the paper looking for a natural feature and a low elevation that would suggest a canyon.

He found a narrow sliver and gauged the distance on the scale below.

If he was correct, Vera was a good hour's drive away. He made a notation of the exact longitude and latitude and typed the GPS location into his phone, as it would be impossible to utilize natural landmarks to guide him in the dark.

For all he knew, Vera might be on her way back and wasn't picking up her phone because she was driving.

Or maybe, she had broken down on the road and was stranded.

Either way, he had to be sure.

Damn it Vera, don't you know I have enough to worry about.

33

BUTTING HEADS

Roxy raced up the cement stairs to the second floor and pounded on Ethan and Kane's apartment door. When no one answered, she tried the doorknob and found it unlocked. She pushed open the door and stepped into the shabby living room. The place was a shambles; dirty clothes strewn across a couch and an armchair with stuffing jutting out where the fabric was ripped; empty beer bottles and discarded takeout containers on the coffee table.

"Damn it, Ethan! Where are you?" Roxy yelled, kicking a boot across the carpet.

"Hey, hey," Ethan said, coming out of his room. He wore a wrinkly pair of boxer shorts and looked like he had just woken up.

"Why did you do it?"

"What are you talking about?" Ethan grimaced, nursing a hangover.

"You know what I'm talking about," Roxy shouted.

"You mean the bar? What was I supposed to do, the jack-off pulled a knife."

"Wait. What happened at the bar?"

Ethan collapsed on the couch. "We had a little trouble. We took care of it."

"I'm talking about Macy."

"What about her? She didn't get hurt."

"That's where you're wrong. Macy's dead."

Ethan sat up straight on the couch. "What?"

"That's why I was reaming you on the phone."

"But why didn't you tell me then? I had no idea why you were mad."

"Because I wanted to see your face when you denied it," Roxy said. "How could you do it?"

"I would never hurt Macy, you know that. I love her."

Roxy paced about the room. "Shit, shit! Damn it, Ethan. How many times have I told you to keep it under control?"

"But I didn't kill her," Ethan said.

"How do I know? Each time, you swear you don't remember what happened."

"Then arrest me."

"What?"

"You heard me. Take me in."

"I can't do that."

"Why not?"

"Because this isn't just all about you, that's why," Roxy said.

"Take me in, Roxy." Ethan stood up and put his hands out in front of him for Roxy to throw on the handcuffs.

"No!"

"What, do I have to give you a reason?" Ethan thrust out his right arm and punched Roxy in the shoulder, catapulting her across the room, and slamming her against the wall.

Roxy slid down onto the floor. She glared up at Ethan. "Don't, I'm warning you."

Ethan curled his upper lip.

Roxy could see the fangs jut out of his mouth. The whites of his eyes yellowed and his pupils narrowed into slits. Coarse black hair emerged out of his human skin, covering his body with a mat of short fur. Ethan's nose elongated into a long snout and his ears sprouted out from the sides of his head as his bones cracked and his body went through its transformation. His nails became thick, extending out from his fingertips into lethal claws.

Standing upright, Ethan's animal-self was a crossbreed of lupine and wolverine.

Roxy stared at the abomination that only seconds ago had been her brother. She knew her gun would be useless and regular bullets couldn't stop him. If he came at her, there was a way to kill him. She prayed he still had some presence of mind. "Stay here and don't you leave." She backed across the room and slowly opened the front door.

Ethan watched her intently.

Stepping outside, Roxy closed the door behind her. She could hear Ethan on the other side of the door, snarling as he tore up the place.

Roxy ran down the stairs. She climbed into the Mustang and drove out of the parking lot.

34

INCENDIARY DUD

Ben kept trying to reach Vera on the phone while he drove but wasn't successful. Finally, he gave up and returned the display back to the GPS app tracking the location of the box canyon. He gazed out through the windshield at the desert ahead, brightly lit up by the Tahoe's high beams and the halogen spotlights on the roof rack. If his hunch was correct, finding Vera wouldn't be a problem.

Glancing down at the tiny screen on his phone, he could see that he was almost there. But when he looked up, his heart sank. He slammed on the brakes short of colliding with the barrier of rocks blocking the entrance to the canyon.

"Now what?" Ben let the engine idle as he contemplated what he should do. It was obvious she hadn't gone this way. "Damn!" Frustrated, Ben slammed the center of the steering wheel and the horn blared. He was about to grab the gearshift and put the Tahoe in reverse, when he heard a car horn answer back.

Ben hit the horn again.

This time the reply was a series of blasts.

"Thank God," Ben said. He turned off the engine, grabbed a flashlight, and got out of his vehicle. He shined his light on the rocks and began to climb. Once he reached the top, he could see Vera's Jeep below on the other side. He panned the beam on her rear window and could see her sitting up front in the cab.

"Hey! Are you all right?" he called out. He directed the light on the rocks in front of him so he wouldn't step wrong and fall. While he was busy looking at his feet, he could hear something flying above his head.

The driver's-side door on the Jeep flew open. Vera stepped out and yelled, "Ben! Look out!" She pointed up at the night sky.

Ben leaned back and shined the flashlight straight up.

The sudden glare caught the hideous creature by surprise. Hovering only ten feet above Ben's head, it looked like a demonic gargoyle with massive teeth and four pointy-clawed feet. Shaking its head, it shrieked and flew off to escape the bright light. But it wasn't alone because Ben could hear the echoing of fluttering wings bouncing off the canyon walls.

He rushed down the rocks. Slipping, he fell, but got right up. He yelled to Vera, "Get back in," and when she crossed over to the passenger seat, he jumped in and shut the door.

And not a second too soon as a creature slammed into the side window, cracking the glass.

"What happened?" Ben said. "Did you run out of gas?"

"No! I didn't run out of gas," Vera replied, indignantly. "There's a hole in the oil pan. And what the hell are those things?"

"I think they're chupacabras. Once in a while we'd get a call, a rancher or camper claiming they'd seen one of these creatures but I always thought it was someone pulling a prank. I can't believe these things really exist."

Another flying chupacabra flung its body at the side panel of the Jeep. Soon there was a flock of them, battering the outside of the vehicle like a mass of lost migratory birds flying blindly into a cliff wall.

Vera put her hands over her head, expecting at any moment for the creatures to break through the glass. "What do we do?"

Ben kept flashing his light into their faces; each time getting the same reaction. They were definitely creatures of the night and hated bright light. "Did you bring a flashlight?"

"Yeah."

"They must be nocturnal. Probably don't like sunlight. We could use our flashlights to scare them back while we make it to the Tahoe."

"You really think that's going to work?"

Ben figured there had to be twenty or more out there. Surely they wouldn't be able to blind all of them. They needed something really bright. He looked over his shoulder at the back seat and saw Vera's paint supplies. "What if we can make a torch?"

While Vera grabbed her sweatshirt, Ben reached back and snapped a leg off the easel. He used the sleeves and tied the sweatshirt around the shank of wood. "Did you bring any paint thinner?"

"Yes, right here." Vera found a pint can of solvent.

"Good. Now pour some on. Try not to breathe it in," Ben instructed.

Vera saturated the sweatshirt with the mineral spirits. The cab began to smell like the interior of an automotive paint shop. She reached in the glove compartment and took out a box of survivor matches.

"These matches are the kind that don't go out even if you dunk them in water," Ben said. "Which gives me an idea."

He took a match out of the box. It was storm-proof and thicker than a no. 2 pencil. Once lit, the flame was impossible to put out and would burn for 15 seconds. "Grab me a paint tube and we'll insert the match, make our own version of a Molotov cocktail."

Vera reached behind the seat and handed Ben a tube of paint.

Ben removed the cap, and inserted the long match into the tube. He ran the striker across the head of the match, rolled down the glass, and lobbed the fiery tube out the window.

The improvised Molotov cocktail landed on the ground and burned ineffectively like a road flare about to go out.

"That was a dud," Vera said.

"The hell with it. Let's go!" Ben opened the door and lit the torch. The sweatshirt made a *poof* when it ignited. He jumped out, waited for Vera, and they climbed up the loose rock, Ben holding the torch up high like a primitive explorer.

When they got to the Tahoe, Ben threw the torch on the ground and they got safely inside. He started the engine and looked over at Vera. "You okay?"

"I am now." She reached over and squeezed his hand.

"Wait a second," Ben said, suddenly realizing something. "Weren't you out here to paint something? What happened to it?"

"I'm afraid my golden opportunity upped and flew away," Vera said.

35

THE HEALING ROOM

Camilla rushed up the porch steps and opened the front door for Miguel so he could carry Maria inside the house.

"Where to?" Miguel asked, stepping into the living room.

"In the back," Camilla said. She led the way down the hall. She opened a door and switched on a hanging glass lamp to a backroom that once was a bedroom but was now converted to a parlor. Camilla pointed to a divan covered with Navajo blankets. "Put her there."

Miguel stepped over and lay Maria on the couch. His wife was unconscious and wore a bandage that Camilla had ripped from her skirt and wrapped around the top of Maria's head. He turned and saw Sophia weeping in the doorway.

"Papa, is Momma going to wake up?"

Miguel came over and hugged Sophia. "Everything's going to be fine." He watched his mother go about the room, lighting candles and sticks of incense.

A round table and four wooden chairs were set up in the middle of the room like one would expect to see used by a fortuneteller or for a small gathering for a séance.

The walls were covered with dreamcatchers made of feathers and beads, a few oil paintings of warrior braves on horseback, leather tack, some Native American arrows and bows, and wooden masks painted with scary faces. Next to the burning candles on the shelves were pottery bowls used for grinding herbs and an assortment of Pueblo flageolets and rawhide drums.

Miguel felt something brush by his leg. He looked down and saw Astuto scamper into the room. He was carrying a mug, the contents sloshing over the rim.

"Careful there," Camilla said.

Astuto handed her the cup.

"What is that?" Sophia asked. "A magic potion?"

"No, child. It's water." Camilla knelt beside Maria and raised her head. She poured a little water over Maria's lips.

"What can we do?" Miguel asked.

"Right now? It is best you wait outside. Let me heal her."

"Please don't let her..." but then Miguel clammed up, not wanting to further upset Sophia or insult his mother by suggesting her shaman powers might fail. He placed his hand on Sophia's shoulder. "Let's do as Abuela says. We should check on the animals."

"Okay," Sophia replied in a low voice.

As they walked toward the living room, Miguel glanced over his shoulder and saw the small troll push the door closed.

Passing through the house, Miguel could hear his mother chanting in the back room. He opened the front door and let Sophia go out first.

That's when they heard the goats cry out.

"Papa, what is it?"

"I don't believe it. They must have followed us."

36

SKINWALKER

Ben dimmed the headlights and switched off the rooftop halogens when he saw their driveway up ahead. He glanced over at Vera. She seemed less frazzled since their terrifying ordeal with the chupacabras.

"Tomorrow I'll see about getting the Jeep towed," Ben said, turning down the driveway.

"You really think they'll be able—BEN, LOOK OUT!"

A large animal darted out in front of the Tahoe.

Ben slammed on the brakes. He turned to see where it went but it vanished into the dark. "What was it? A mule deer?"

"I don't think so. It was running on two legs," Vera said.

"Are you sure?"

"I know what I saw."

Ben stared out the window expecting whatever it was to reappear but it didn't. He put his foot back on the accelerator and drove slowly to the front of the garage. He pressed the remote on the visor, raising the garage door.

They got out of the Tahoe, entered through the garage, and went inside the house.

"I could use a drink," Vera said as they came into the living room.

"I'll make us both one," Ben said. "Let me check if there are any messages on the machine. I was supposed to meet Monroe at his office."

"Why's that?"

"Macy Brown was murdered."

"My God," Vera said. "That's terrible. What happened?"

"She was attacked at work. We think it might have been a large predator. I should give him a call and reschedule for tomorrow." Ben walked over to the kitchen counter. He picked up the phone and punched in the coroner's number.

Vera walked over and opened the sliding glass door.

"What are you doing?" Ben asked.

"I left some things out on the deck."

"Maybe you should wait," Ben warned, but she had already stepped out on to the deck, triggering the automatic security lights. Monroe's voicemail came on asking the caller to leave a message. Ben made it short.

Vera came back inside carrying a can of paintbrushes and a half-finished canvas of a sunrise in progress. She put everything on the coffee table.

"Better close the door," Ben said, placing the phone back on the dock.

Just then a bright light shined into the room.

"Looks like we have a visitor," Vera said, stepping into the kitchen and looking out the window at the headlights coming down the driveway.

"Who is it?" Ben asked.

"It's your deputy. What's she doing here?"

"I don't know."

Vera turned.

A wolf-like creature covered in dark fur was in the open doorway. It stood upright and was six feet tall, the lower parts of the hind legs reversed like the stifle and hock on a canine. Black marble eyes, ears perked high on the sides of its enormous head, staring at them with a permanent sneer so as to show off its long pointy fangs and a mouthful of savage teeth on its protruded snout. It had broad shoulders, a massive chest, and muscular arms. Sharp claws extended from the front paws like menacing kitchen knives.

And that's when Vera screamed.

* * *

Roxy pulled up to the Lobo's home. She shut off the Mustang's engine and turned off the lights. After her blowout with Ethan, she had swung by the Coroner's Office thinking Ben was going to meet her there but he never showed up. Monroe had done a visual evaluation of Macy Brown's body with the actual autopsy planned for tomorrow morning but wanted to share his notes with Ben and had asked Roxy if she would give Ben a copy.

She grabbed the one-page preliminary report and got out of the cruiser. She went up to the front door and was about to ring the bell when she heard a woman scream inside like she was auditioning for a horror film.

Instead of trying to kick in the front door, Roxy drew her weapon and dashed down the wraparound deck to the back.

She stepped into the house and saw Vera standing in the kitchen, her back against the refrigerator; Ben with his service revolver drawn, in the middle of the living room, five feet away from a wolf-like beast standing on its hind legs.

"What the hell is it?" Vera gasped.

"I don't know." Ben cocked his weapon.

"Don't shoot," Roxy said.

The creature turned when it heard her voice.

"What do you mean don't shoot?" Ben said.

"You can't kill it," Roxy replied.

"Are you serious?" Vera said.

The beast looked back at Ben. It flashed its fangs, a guttural growl rumbling in its chest.

"Not with lead bullets," Roxy said.

"What?" Vera asked.

"It's a Nagual," Roxy said, further clarifying by saying, "a shapeshifter."

The skinwalker snarled and lurched across the floor.

Ben fired a single shot. The bullet grazed the side of the creature's head, severing its left ear and sending bloody bits of fur flying in the air.

The Nagual roared, and with one powerful swipe, raked Ben's forearm and wrist with its sharp claws, propelling the gun out of the sheriff's hand.

Ben fell back into the kitchen, eyes locked on his ravaged arm, blood dripping onto the floor in big splats.

Vera grabbed a dishtowel off the oven door handle and rushed over to Ben, wrapping the cloth around the gaping wounds.

The skinwalker came at Ben and Vera.

"Stop!" Roxy yelled at the creature. "One more step and I swear I'll..."

The beast halted and stared back at Roxy. Their eyes locked. Roxy knew that a skinwalker's greatest fear was to have its human name said aloud whenever it was residing in its animal-self because it meant sure death.

As if summoned suddenly by an audible command that only it could hear, the creature bolted across the room, leaped out onto the deck, and ran off into the night.

Ben and Vera stared at Roxy.

"You knew about that thing?" Vera asked.

"I can explain," Roxy said.

"Okay," Vera said. "Then start by explaining what just happened."

Ben's legs gave out and he slipped to the floor. The heels of his boots skidded on the blood-soaked tiles.

Vera grabbed another dishtowel and wrapped it tightly around his forearm.

"Before we get into it, Ben needs that arm patched up," Roxy said, hoisting Ben to his feet. Vera put her arm round Ben's waist and they staggered out of the house to the Mustang.

37

BLOODSUCKING BASTARDS

"Go back in the house," Miguel told Sophia.

"But Papa."

"Now!" Miguel nudged his daughter inside and made sure the front door was closed. He could hear the chupacabras screeching and the animals' fearful cries as they scampered about in their pens behind the house. He had been in such a hurry to get Sophia back in the house that he hadn't thought to grab a gun.

He jumped down off the porch and ran around to the side of the house where his mother's old truck had been left abandoned. All four tires were flat and the bed was full of junk. Miguel reached in and grabbed a four-foot long section of water pipe. He wielded the crude weapon in his hand and took a swing at the truck's already dented fender. The blow split the rusted metal.

Miguel dashed over to the pens. Two chupacabras had the donkey cornered in the corral while four other creatures hunched over the two goats lying on the ground, their mouths clamped on the goats' necks, sucking their blood. Miguel stepped up on a railing and vaulted over the fence. "HEY!" he yelled.

The chupacabras assaulting the donkey turned when they heard Miguel shout.

Using the pipe like a spear, Miguel thrust the pipe into the nearest creature's belly and all the way out its back. The abomination opened its bowl-shaped mouth and shrieked. Miguel yanked the pipe out of its body. Blood and gore dripped out the end of the pipe. He watched the creature drop dead.

He heard another squeal. The other chupacabra was on the ground and was flailing in the dirt, the donkey kicking it repeatedly with its hind hooves. Happy to see the donkey doling out its own brand of punishment, Miguel darted into the goats' pen.

Seeing the vile bloodsuckers feasting on the defenseless goats, and having attacked Maria and nearly abducted Sophia, Miguel went into a rage.

He came at the chupacabras swinging.

The lead pipe cracked open a skull, then bashed in a hideous face. A third swing smashed one in the back, breaking its spine. Before the last chupacabra knew what was happening, Miguel brought the heavy pipe down on its head like an axe striking a wedge in a log, splitting its cranium in half.

He heard a noise behind him and spun around.

Astuto stood on the top railing of the fence. He was poised, ready to fight with his knife in his tiny hand. He looked from one dead chupacabra to another lying on the ground, each time his wrinkled face showing more disappointment.

"Sorry," Miguel said to the troll. "Next time I'll leave you some. Come on and I'll show you how to change a tire."

38

SILVER BULLETS

Roxy and Vera were asked to wait in the lobby while an ER doctor and a nurse wheeled Ben back to the trauma center. Roxy took a seat in a chair while Vera paced the room. It was close to midnight and there were no other people in the lobby.

"Okay, let's hear it," Vera said.

Roxy looked up at Vera with a blank expression.

"That thing! What was it again?"

"I told you," Roxy said. "It was a Nagual."

"What, like a werewolf?"

"Not exactly, but close. It's a person that can take on an animal form."

"How is that even possible? That only happens in the movies."

"Believe me; it's real."

"How do you know?"

"I just know," Roxy said.

"So you know who that creature is?"

Roxy didn't answer.

"Well? Do you?"

"I have to go," Roxy said and stood up.

"Where're you going?" Vera asked venomously.

"There's something I have to do. I'll call later to see how Ben's doing."

"What is it you're not telling me?" Vera said raising her voice but by then Roxy was already running out the open automatic doors to her cruiser parked at the curb.

* * *

When Roxy got to the housing complex, she found the door to Ethan and Kane's apartment left ajar. Which meant Ethan had gone out as she was certain she had closed it when she had last been there. She peered through the narrow opening. The front room was dark.

"Ethan?" She could hear rustling inside. She stepped back away from the door.

Drawing her service weapon, Roxy ejected the clip filled with lead rounds and substituted it with a clip from her belt that contained silver bullets. She ratcheted a bullet in the chamber. She used the toe of her boot to edge the door open and stepped inside.

Even though the room was dark as a cave, she could see the silhouette of someone sitting on the couch.

Roxy felt along the wall. She found a light switch and turned it on. A lamp on top of an end table came on, shining on Ethan.

"Why, Ethan?" She pointed her gun at her brother.

"Why what?" Ethan said.

"Why couldn't you just stay here like I told you?"

"I did. I guess I made a mess of things."

"Quit lying to me." Roxy took another step and her boot crunched on something made of glass.

"I'm not. I've been here the whole time."

"Liar."

"You know what, Roxy? Screw you! I'm sick and tired of your bullshit. Thinking you're so much better than me because you work for the sheriff. The hell with you! Just leave me alone!"

"Ethan, you have to stop!" She could hear his breathing becoming raspy and knew he was about to change.

"Yeah? Then stop me!" Ethan lunged from the couch and came at Roxy.

"Ethan, no!" Roxy yelled, firing a quick succession of shots. Ethan howled and collapsed facedown on the carpet at her feet.

"Jesus, Roxy, what did you do?"

Roxy spun around and saw a figure standing in the front doorway.

It was Kane, dressed in a dark T-shirt and jeans, the Colt revolver on his hip, the left side of his face caked in blood, missing an ear.

39

BROTHERLY HATE

"My God, it was *you*?" Roxy said, feeling her body deflate, knowing she had just killed her brother for nothing.

"Yeah," Kane said, "and thanks to you, the sheriff's still alive."

"What, you went there to kill him? But why?"

"With him out of the way, I was planning to move in on his wife. So, where is he now, the clinic?"

"That's right, you son of a bitch."

"Watch what you say, little sister." Kane stepped into the front room. He looked down at Ethan's body. "So how are you going to explain your way out of this? Looks like you screwed the pooch."

Roxy tapped her temple with the barrel of her pistol and began to cry. "I was trying to protect him. Even after what he did to those people out in the desert and Macy Brown."

"What makes you think it was Ethan?" Kane said smugly.

"You mean..."

"And you call yourself a detective."

"Damn you, Kane!" Roxy raised her pistol.

Kane drew his Colt revolver and pumped three bullets into her chest.

40

THAT HAD TO HURT

"Holy shit, did you hear that?" Kyle said.

"It was on the TV," Christy said, stepping out of the kitchen with a bowl of popcorn in her hands.

"Gunshots on Wheel of Fortune?" Kyle muted Pat Sajak questioning a contestant. "That came from next door."

"Should we call the police?"

"Not a good idea," Kyle said, directing her attention to the coffee table cluttered with a bong and a glass pipe, bags of weeds, and other drug paraphernalia. "Shit, you don't think someone went and made off with Ethan's stash do you?"

"Great, there goes our supply," Christy said.

"We have to go over there."

"Are you insane?"

"Come on, before the place becomes a gong show." Kyle got up from his recliner, rushed over to the door, and stepped outside onto the railed walkway that stretched along the front of the second-floor apartments.

Christy placed the bowl of popcorn on the coffee table and came out to join Kyle. She looked down at the gloomy parking lot below and the shadowy figures making transactions. "We should go back inside. I don't like being out here after dark."

"Just come on," Kyle said.

They walked warily to the next apartment and found the door standing open.

Kyle and Christy peered inside and saw two bodies on the floor.

"I told you I heard shots," Kyle said. "Believe me now?"

"My God, is that Ethan?" Christy gasped.

"Yeah," Kyle said, stepping into the room. He knelt to take a closer look at Ethan and noticed the man clutching a Colt revolver.

"Is he dead?"

"Oh yeah."

"Is that a cop?"

Kyle walked over and stood over the woman lying face up on the carpet. "Man, this is crazy. It's his sister. The sheriff deputy."

"What do you think happened?" Christy asked.

"They must have gotten into a beef and shot each other. Watch the door."

"Why? What are you going to do?"

"Just watch the damn door." Kyle dashed into the back rooms. He came back fifteen seconds later, carrying a large paper sack.

"My God, Kyle."

"Shut up. Let's get out of here." Kyle bent down beside Ethan's sister.

"Jesus, Kyle, *now* what are you doing?"

Kyle picked the deputy's service weapon off the floor. He waved it in the air like it was a trophy he had just won. "This is so cool."

"Put it back you idiot!"

"No way, it's mine now."

Ethan's sister sat up suddenly and sucked in a deep breath, scaring the shit out of Christy and Kyle. The deputy grabbed the front of her uniform shirt with both hands, and ripped it open, popping buttons onto the carpet. Next she spread apart the Velcro straps on her Kevlar bulletproof vest. Shrugging out of it, she pulled her T-shirt up over her bra and stared down at the two welts positioned over her cleavage, another bruise above her belly button.

She looked up, saw Kyle holding her gun, and growled, "DROP IT ASSHOLE BEFORE I TEAR YOUR DAMN HEAD OFF!"

41

TRUAMA UNIT

It took Miguel awhile to hike back to the truck, change the flat tire, and return to the house. Camilla was waiting for him, standing on the porch while Maria and Sophia sat on the swing. A fresh bandage had been applied to Maria's head. She looked like she had just woken up, slumped against Sophia with her eyes glazed over.

"How is she?" Miguel asked, getting out of the truck.

"I think she's up for the ride," his mother replied.

Miguel rushed up the steps. "Come on, we're going to get you checked over." He lifted Maria off the porch swing and carried her down to the truck. He sat her on the seat and fastened her seatbelt.

Camilla and Sophia climbed into the back.

Before Miguel could get behind the wheel, Astuto appeared out of nowhere and jumped up on the seat. Miguel looked to his mother. "Is it okay if he comes?"

"Sure, why not."

Astuto scrunched up next to Maria like a pet dog protecting its master.

It was a thirty-minute ride to the medical clinic. Soon as they pulled up to the Emergency entrance, Miguel got out of the truck and rushed into the lobby. He grabbed one of the patient wheelchairs parked by the door and pushed it out to the truck.

As it was early morning and still dark, Miguel didn't see any harm in leaving the truck where it was and they all went inside. Camilla went up to the window and spoke with a nurse while Miguel and Sophia stood beside Maria in the wheelchair. The only other person in the lobby was a woman reading a magazine on the other side of the room.

Miguel spotted the mischievous troll poking his head out from behind a potted plant a few feet away. "You better stay out of trouble," he whispered.

Astuto scampered across the floor, ducking behind a couch.

"Poppa, I'm hungry," Sophia said.

Miguel noticed a vending machine next to the entry doors leading into the trauma unit. He took out his wallet, fished out two dollars, and handed the bills to Sophia. "Here you go."

Sophia skipped over to the vending machine. Astuto peered around the end of the couch to see what Sophia was doing.

A nurse opened the door leading into the clinic and called out, "Vera Lobo!"

"That's me," said the woman reading the magazine. She got up and followed the nurse into the back.

Miguel dropped to one knee so he could talk to Maria. "How are you feeling?"

Maria had been staring at the floor. She turned her head slowly and faced Miguel.

"Did I die?"

A chill came over Miguel. "What? No. Why would you say that?"

"Do you recall when you told me about your father, how he suffered from sleep apnea?"

"Yeah, but what does that have to do with you?" Miguel asked, growing concerned.

"Remember that one time he woke up in the middle of the night?"

"Yeah, he said his heart had stopped and he wasn't breathing. It was like he wasn't connected to his body. He felt no sensation whatsoever."

"That's how I was back at your mother's. I think I died."

"What? That's absurd."

"Is it? Your mother brought me back to life."

"What, CPR?"

"I don't think that was it. I think she used one of her healing spells."

"Maria, you and I both know—"

"I'm telling you, it's true!" Tears streaked down Maria's cheeks.

"Then it's a miracle," Miguel said and squeezed her hand.

Maria took a moment and glanced about the lobby. "So why are we here?"

"You need stitches." Miguel saw Sophia returning with two candy bars.

"Here Poppa, I got you and me an Almond Joy."

"Thank you," Miguel said. He looked at Maria. "Want to split it?"

Maria shook her head.

Miguel watched Astuto sneak up on Sophia. As soon as she unwrapped her candy bar, the troll reached up and snatched one of the pieces.

"Hey, give that back!"

The troll stuffed the chocolate in its mouth and scurried behind a row of chairs.

Camilla walked over. "They're ready for Maria."

"Did they say if I could go in with her?"

"You can. I'll wait out here with Sophia and make sure Astuto stays out of trouble."

Miguel grabbed the handles on the wheelchair and steered Maria to the doorway where a nurse was already waiting. They went in and followed a hallway to an area where another patient was lying on a gurney. By the uniform, Miguel figured he was the sheriff. A pile of bloody gauze was on the floor. The ER doctor was threading catgut to close up the man's arm while the woman that had been in the lobby watched from a chair.

"I'm almost done," the doctor said over his shoulder.

"We can go in here." The nurse opened a curtain to the adjacent patient area.

The nurse and Miguel helped Maria out of the wheelchair and onto the gurney.

"So how were you injured?" the nurse asked Maria.

"We were in a car accident," Miguel said. "Maria struck her head."

The nurse looked at Maria for confirmation.

"I hit my head, yes," Maria said.

"Where's the restroom?" Miguel asked.

"Through the double doors, down the hall, and to the right," the nurse said.

"I won't be long." Miguel kissed Maria on the forehead and went in search of the restroom.

He went through the double doors and saw the nurse that had been talking with Camilla, sitting at a desk behind the counter at the nursing station. A custodian was at the opposite end of the corridor, pushing a pail by the mop handle. Counting the ER doctor and the nurse with Maria, that made a skeleton crew of four people working the graveyard shift.

Miguel glanced in the half dozen rooms as he went by and saw only one patient occupying a bed. The young man was sleeping. He had a bandage on his head and his right leg was suspended in a sling.

Miguel hoped Maria would be allowed to leave after she was treated and the doctor didn't insist she stay for observation and additional tests. There was no telling what the results might reveal.

He spotted the sign over the men's room and pushed open the door.

42

NO REGRETS

Kane pulled his truck around back to the rear parking lot behind the medical clinic. He saw only three vehicles. He parked at the far end next to a hedgerow that ran along the backside of the building.

He felt no remorse shooting his sister. Even less framing his brother, planting the Colt revolver in Ethan's hand. After an extensive search of the apartment—and finding the drugs Kane had hidden in Ethan's room—it would become apparent that the two dead bodies were a result of a botched drug bust. Finally he was done worrying about his brother's inability to control himself and Roxy always breathing down his neck.

Guess I am a cold-hearted bastard, he thought to himself.

He sat in the cab pondering what he should do next, knowing it wouldn't be smart entering through the front lobby with all those cameras. The rear door to the building was twenty feet away.

Kane's entire body suddenly electrified with pain.

He pushed the handle down to open the truck door a crack.

Kane knew he had little time to undress and immediately pulled his T-shirt up over his head, the joints in his shoulders cracking like thin boards snapped across a knee.

He hurriedly kicked off his boots and frantically unbuckled his belt, undoing the snap on his jeans and yanking them off. The bones in his arms and legs elongated, stretching his muscles beyond human limits. He gripped the steering wheel and watched sharp claws steadily poking out of the ends of his thick, hairy fingers.

The agonizing change took twenty seconds.

* * *

Randy Cameron knew it was nowhere near his break time but he needed a cigarette. Work was the only time he smoked as his wife called it a dirty habit and always got after him to quit. Someday, he swore to her he would; just not now.

He pushed the bucket of sudsy water with the mop handle and walked it down the hall to the glass door leading out to the back parking lot. Like a fool, he had forgotten his employee ID badge at home. The badge had a magnetic strip, that when swiped through one of the electronic card readers mounted at the entry doors, allowed him into the building.

Luckily, when he had come to work, he had been able to piggyback with one of the nurses after she ran her card and followed her into the clinic.

Randy pushed the bar, opening the door and stepped outside. Because the door would automatically lock, he propped it open with the bucket.

He rummaged in his shirt pocket and found he had only one cigarette in the wrinkled soft pack. When he went to put it to his lips, he saw tobacco sticking out of the paper in the middle. He broke the damaged cigarette in half, figuring he best save it for his next break, as there wasn't a cigarette machine in the building.

He dug a Bic lighter out of his trouser pocket and lit up the stubby cigarette. He leaned against the wall and took a deep drag, expelling a plume of smoke up into the night air. Two more puffs and the damn thing was burning his fingers. He dropped the smoldering butt on the walkway and grinded it out with the sole of his shoe.

Opening the door wider, he grabbed the top of the mop handle, and pushed the bucket inside. He had only gone a few steps when he stopped, sensing something was wrong when he didn't hear the door close behind him.

Randy turned and nearly crapped his pants. "Ah, Jesus!"

He stepped back, still clutching the mop handle. His heart pounded in his chest like a manic fist was attempting to beat its way out. He couldn't believe his eyes.

The door closed and in stepped a werewolf.

The lycanthrope snarled, displaying its fanged teeth, thin ropey drool dripping off its chin. It was covered in a thick mat of black fur. Randy could tell by the way it moved that it was extremely strong.

Randy's first instinct was to run like hell, but knew if he did, the monstrous beast would be on him in a flash.

The werewolf stared at Randy like he was a scrumptious feast and took a menacing step toward him.

Randy grabbed the mop, kicked the bucket over, and dumped soapy water all over the floor. He wielded the feeble mop head in front of him.

With one quick swipe, the powerful werewolf snapped the long stick in half, leaving Randy with an unimposing piece of wood in his hand.

This time, Randy didn't think twice; he turned and ran.

He glanced over his shoulder and saw the werewolf slipping and sliding on the wet floor. In its frustration, the beast snatched the bucket, threw it back over its shoulder, and smashed out the glass in the door.

Upon getting its traction, the werewolf roared and loped down the hall.

By then Randy had made it around the corner and was running like a crazy man.

43

STIR CRAZY

Billy Wilkins woke up wishing he had listened to his buddies and girlfriend when they told him not to jump his dirt bike over that ditch. Now look at him. Confined in a hospital bed with a shattered tibia, his right leg suspended in a sling hanging on a long bar that stretched the length of the bed, not to mention a cracked skull with a concussion.

And if that wasn't bad enough, he'd heard the doctor tell his parents they were planning to transfer him tomorrow where they planned to insert a steel pin in his leg.

Which meant no more crazy stunts. Yeah right. As soon as he was able to get back on his feet he'd be back on his bike. Never stopped his idol, Evil Knievel, one of the best stunt riders of all time.

Lying in bed, he was bored out of his mind having nothing to do. Hell, he couldn't even get up to go to the bathroom. It was humiliating having to use a bedpan, especially when that pretty nurse would have to come in and empty his crap into the toilet. He still couldn't look her in the eye.

He glanced over at the copies of *Dirt Bike* and *Motocross Action Magazine* his mother had brought him from home, piled on the table next to the hospital bed. He must have read them a million times.

He was going absolutely stir crazy.

Boy, what he wouldn't do for just a little bit of excitement.

A man bolted into his room and closed the door.

"Who are you?"

"Randy, the night janitor. Keep your voice down!"

"Why? What's going on?" Billy asked, somewhat intrigued.

Randy peered out the small window on the door. "Shit, here it comes!" He looked around the room. "I need to block the door." He ran over, grabbed the footboard, and spun the hospital bed around.

The jarring movement caused the splintered bones in Billy's shin to grind together, causing him extreme pain. "Oh my God, what are you doing?" Billy screamed.

"Stop screaming," Randy snapped. He went around, grabbed the headboard, and shoved the bed across the floor, banging it into the door.

Again, Billy screamed like his balls were on fire. Pausing to suck in a deep breath, Billy saw a face in the window. Not a human face but a wolf's face. How could that possibly be? That would mean the animal had to be standing on its hind legs to see into his room. "What the...what the hell is that?"

"It's a werewolf!"

"What are you even saying?" Billy cried. "There's no such—"

Then came a loud bang and the door opened a crack. A large hairy arm reached in but quickly pulled back out when Randy rammed the bed against the door.

Billy screamed. A sadistic torturer couldn't have inflected near the same amount of pain even if he had cleaved Billy's shin with a machete and poured a pound of rock salt into the wound. Billy slammed his head back onto the pillow and blubbered, "Please stop."

Randy rushed over to the door and peeked out the window. "I don't see it." He looked from another angle. "I think it's gone." He turned around.

"Get the nurse," Billy said. "Please, I need something for the pain."

"I'm not going out there. Use your call button."

"I can't reach it. You moved the bed."

"Well, I'm not budging from this door," Randy said. "What if that thing comes back?"

Billy screamed so loud his vocal cords snapped.

44

SPILLED COFFEE

Miguel was in the restroom, washing his hands at the sink, when he heard the first muffled scream. He pulled a paper towel from the dispenser, wiped his hands, and made his way to the door. He stuck his head out and glanced both ways before stepping out into the hall. It sounded more like a man than a woman so the first thought that came to mind was the scream came from the patient he'd seen laid up in his room.

Rushing down the hall, Miguel heard another god-awful scream that ended abruptly like someone had suddenly placed a hand over the person's mouth. This time he was sure it was the young man.

When he reached the room, he found the door closed. He gave it a push. It wasn't locked because it opened slightly but something was preventing him from opening it all the way. "Hey, everything okay in there?" Miguel said. "Was that you screaming?"

"Yes," the young man replied hoarsely.

"How come I can't open the door?"

"That's because I'm blocking it with the bed," another man's voice said.

"Who are you?" Miguel asked.

"The night janitor."

"Then open the door."

"Screw that! Not with that thing out there."

"What thing?"

"It's a werewolf. If I were you, I'd get the hell out of there."

Miguel had no idea what the man was talking about. He stepped away from the door and looked down the hall at the nursing station. He wondered why the nurse on duty hadn't responded to the young man's screams. He went down the corridor to find out why.

"Excuse me, Nurse?" Miguel said, walking up to the counter. "I think the patient down the hall needs your help."

He looked over and saw medical folders strewn about the floor. The chair behind the desk was lying on its side like someone had knocked it over trying to scramble out of it. Spilt coffee was all over the desk and on the floor. Miguel saw a shoe print in a puddle. He glanced across the hall and saw a closed door.

Miguel went over and tried the handle. He pushed the door open a few inches but then it stopped abruptly. "What is it with this place and doors?" He reached in, and when he turned on the light switch on the wall, he heard a gasp.

"Someone in here?" Miguel asked.

"Thank God," a woman's voice replied, and opened the door. It was the night nurse. Her mascara was streaked from crying and the front of her white uniform was badly stained where she had spilled coffee on herself. She looked so happy to see him, he thought she might throw her arms around his neck and give him a kiss.

"What happened? I saw the mess at your desk."

"It came at me so fast. I jumped out of my chair and ran in here."

"What came at you?"

"I don't know. All I can tell you was that it was big and hairy."

"Don't tell me. A werewolf?"

"My God, now that you mention it, yes. That's exactly what it was."

Miguel could discount one person's crazy claim, but not two. He had to make sure Maria was safe. "Okay, you wait in here. I'll call the police."

"Good luck with that. The Sheriff's in the other room getting stitched up."

A scream came from the examining room.

This time it was a woman.

Miguel dashed for the double doors.

45

ABDUCTION

"Hi, I'm Doctor Clarkson. If you could sit up for me, I can take a look at your head. Are you feeling any dizziness, blurred vision?"

"No, nothing like that," Maria answered. Even though she still felt strange—not every day you got resurrected from the dead—she wasn't sure how much information she should divulge to the doctor.

She sat up and swung her feet over the edge of the gurney. The doctor stepped around to examine the back of her head. She could feel his gloved fingers prodding through her sticky hair.

The double doors banged open and the woman screamed on the other side of the curtain. Maria heard heavy footfalls, not someone wearing shoes, but the sound of a large animal's paws stomping across the floor.

"What in the world?" The doctor threw open the curtain.

A wolf-like beast was about to attack the sheriff lying on the gurney in the next examining area.

"Hey!" the doctor yelled.

The creature cocked its head in the doctor's direction. It marched over, grabbed the physician by the lapels of his lab coat, and hoisted him off his feet.

"Everyone get the hell out of here!" the sheriff shouted, struggling to sit up on the gurney.

Maria saw that his right arm was bandaged. She also noticed that there wasn't a gun in his holster.

The double doors blasted open and Miguel rushed in.

"Miguel, watch out!" shouted Maria.

The beast heard Miguel come in and gave him a quick glance before opening its mouth wide and setting its sharp teeth into the doctor's throat. It tossed back its head and ripped out a long strand of flesh. Blood squirted out of the gaping wound. The wolf-like creature released the doctor, dropping his limp body to the floor.

The sheriff managed to slip off the gurney, using the bed on wheels as a barrier between him and the fierce creature.

Maria watched Miguel get behind a supply cart and push it with all his might, ramming it into the animal's legs. The beast let out a pitiful cry then shoved the cart up against the wall. It turned on Miguel and was about to attack him when the woman who was standing behind the sheriff screamed.

Stepping over the dead doctor, the creature shoved the gurney out of its way and backhanded the sheriff across the face with a powerful blow. The sheriff flew back into the woman and they both crashed against the wall and crumpled to the floor.

Miguel ran over to Maria to protect her from the ferocious animal.

She watched the creature snatch up the semi-conscious woman off the floor and throw her over its shoulder.

The wolf-like beast charged out of the room.

“My God, Miguel,” Maria said. “Did that thing just abduct that woman?”

“Sure as hell looked that way.”

46

NAME CALLING

Camilla was about to get up from her chair and walk around when the door leading from the examining room burst open. As soon as the creature stepped into the lobby she knew it was a Nagual in the animalistic form of a wolf. It had a woman slung over its shoulder: the sheriff's wife, Vera Lobo.

"Oh my God, Abeula," Sophia gasped, sitting in the chair next to her grandmother.

The Nagual glared at Camilla and Sophia like a predator with too many options.

"Don't move, child," Camilla whispered.

Adjusting the passed-out woman on its shoulder, the Nagual stomped toward the automatic doors.

Astuto rushed out from behind a large potted plant. He ran at the shapeshifter and stabbed the beast in the back of the foot with his knife. The Nagual roared and looked down at the tiny troll. A thick blob of drool fell from the beast's gaping mouth and landed on the top of Astuto's head and into his eyes, blinding him.

The beast raised its foot and was about to stomp down on the troll when its attention was drawn to the automatic doors swishing open.

Camilla recognized the figure standing in the doorway even though she was only wearing a T-shirt instead of her uniform shirt. It was the Sheriff's deputy, Roxy Nez, and she was holding a pistol at her side.

"Put her down," Roxy told the creature.

The Nagual snarled and took a step forward.

"I won't tell you again."

It took another step.

"I'm warning you," Roxy said. "Don't make me do it."

The beast didn't comply and kept advancing.

"KANE, STOP!"

The Nagual froze. A strange pitiful look came over its face. Its broad shoulders slumped as though the weight of the woman was too much to bear. Vera Lobo slowly slipped down the back of the beast and onto the floor.

Camilla knew whenever a Nagual was called by its human name, it would soon die a gruesome death. She grabbed Sophia and turned her away. "Cover your eyes, child."

The Nagual leaned back its head and howled at the ceiling. Looking straight at Roxy, it charged the deputy.

Roxy aimed and pulled the trigger multiple times.

Each bullet rocked the Nagual back on its heels as they punched holes in the creature's chest. Camilla knew for the shots to be effective they would have to be tipped with silver.

The deputy kept firing until she emptied her clip.

Dropping to its knees, the Nagual began to change. Its head reverted from canine to an oval shape while its wolf-like body resumed back to human form.

Naked, and riddled with bullets, Kane Nez took his last gasping breath, and fell facedown on the floor.

47

PARTING GIFT

Miguel carried their bags and stowed them in the back of the truck while Sophia and Maria said their goodbyes. He walked back and went up the porch steps. "Well, we're all set."

"I'm going to miss you, Abuela," Sophia said and gave her grandmother a hug.

"And I'm going to miss you, child," Camilla replied, giving Sophia a kiss on the head.

Maria stepped up and gave Camilla an embrace. "Thank you for everything."

Camilla leaned in and whispered something in Maria's ear.

"My turn." Miguel wrapped his arms around his mother and gave her a tender squeeze. "Thank you for having us."

"The pleasure was all mine. Promise to come and see me soon?"

"We will." Miguel stepped back. He glanced over at the corral next to the barn and saw the two goats grazing on some weeds. "Glad to see they're okay."

"They're still a little weak but they'll survive."

Miguel heard the donkey bray from its pen like it knew the Wallas were about to leave and it was saying farewell. Miguel looked at his mother. "You don't think those things will come back?"

"They do, they'll wish they hadn't."

"If there's any trouble, any trouble at all, you call us," Miguel said. "Promise?"

"Yes, son. Don't forget, I *can* take care of myself."

"Just like great-great grandma Lizzy?" Sophia said.

"Just like Lizzy."

"And get that truck of yours fixed," Miguel scolded his mom. "I hate to think of you stranded out here all alone."

"I will. I know someone that owes me a favor. And stop your worrying, I'm never alone. Don't forget I have Astuto and my animals to keep me company."

"Speaking of Astuto, where is the little scoundrel?" Miguel asked.

"Oh, he's somewhere I imagine."

"We should get going."

"Bye," Camilla said.

Sophia ran down the steps. Miguel and Maria followed her to the truck.

"What did my mom whisper in your ear?" Miguel asked Maria when they were far enough away from the house so Camilla wouldn't hear.

"She said 'have a good life.'"

"Well, I guess it's up to me to see that you do," Miguel said and kissed Maria on the cheek. She went around to the passenger side. The door was open. Sophia had already climbed onto the backseat.

Miguel got behind the wheel and was about to close his door when Camilla called out, "Miguel, hold on. Astuto has something for Sophia."

The troll scampered down the porch steps with a gift wrapped in a piece of paper from a plain brown grocery bag and ran across the dirt yard to the truck.

Miguel looked down. "What have you got there?"

The wrinkly-old-man-looking troll held the small package over his head so Miguel could reach it.

"Thank you, my little friend."

Astuto blabbered something and took off running.

"Here you go," Miguel said and handed the present over the seat. Sophia grabbed it and tore through the paper.

"What is it?" Maria asked.

"That little rat," Sophia said and held up her topaz necklace.

Miguel started up the truck. They gave Camilla and Astuto a final wave and drove down the dirt road. "Well, I have to say, that was quite the visit."

"You can say that again," Maria said.

"So when are we coming back?" Sophia asked, putting on her necklace.

"Soon," Miguel said. Her looked over at Maria and she smiled back.

48

CASE SOLVED

Ben sat in the deckchair and gazed out at the panoramic view of the desert, the setting sun casting a burnt orange glow over the sprawling landscape. He grabbed his coffee mug off the armrest and took a sip. Even though he'd washed his favorite cup numerous times, he could still taste a hint of Vera's paint. A constant reminder that his wife would always harbor a jealous streak, especially when it came to Roxy Nez, though after what had transpired in the past few hours, Vera's dislike for Roxy had waned.

After all, the woman did save her life.

"The game hens should be ready in about twenty minutes," Vera said, sitting in the deckchair next to Ben. She raised her wineglass to her lips and drank.

"Great. I'm starved."

"How's the arm?"

"Still throbs."

"Want another pain pill?" Vera asked.

"I'll take one before we sit down to dinner."

"How's the investigation going?"

"With Roxy? Knowing what we've learned about Kane and Ethan, I believe both shootings were justified. I can't imagine what she's going through. I have confidence she'll be cleared to come back to work. Whenever she's ready."

"Guess that's going to leave you a little short-handed."

Ben tried to raise his bandaged arm but stopped when a sharp pain ran up his forearm. "I take it that's your idea of a lame joke?"

"Not as bad as your lame comeback," Vera snickered.

"I had a call this morning from Albuquerque."

"Oh yeah? About what?"

"Remember that art critic that was killed? Brad Filcher?"

"How could I forget? He nearly derailed my career."

"Seems one of the detectives was finally able to get his hands on some decent surveillance footage of the actual murder and was able to get a good look at the killer. Care to take a guess?"

"Who was it?"

"Kane Nez."

49

FRONTIER JUSTICE

Roxy missed being in uniform and driving the Mustang cruiser but there was nothing she could do about it until after the hearing proceedings were complete. She felt confident that she would be cleared of any wrongful doing though it didn't ease the pain knowing she had put both her brothers in the ground. Being on administrative leave gave her the time she needed to deal with her grief.

Though it wasn't her cruiser, Roxy enjoyed her Chevelle SS-396. The paintjob was weathered and the upholstery had rips in places, but it had a Hurst linkage 3-speed transmission with a high-performance small block 350-horsepower V-8 engine, dual glass pack exhaust and ran like a top.

She downshifted into second and turned off the highway into the Quick Stop parking lot. Pulling up to a stall in front of the entrance, Roxy revved the engine, which made the exhaust system rumble and pop. She turned off the ignition and got out of the car.

Even though it was mid-morning, it was already hot. She could feel the sun on her bare shoulders, the heat radiating through the fabric of her tank top and jeans. As soon as the automatic doors opened, she could feel the cool air-conditioning on her face.

Walking into the store, Roxy sensed that something wasn't right when she heard someone groan from behind the checkout stand. She rushed over and looked over the counter. A young man was lying on the floor. He was clutching his side with a bloody hand.

Roxy vaulted over the counter. "Let me help you. I'm a cop."

The young man scrunched up his face and let out a moan.

Raising the bottom of his shirt, Roxy saw that he had been stabbed. "Hold on. You're lucky, it doesn't look too deep." She looked up and saw a paper towel roll on the counter that the clerk probably used to periodically clean the counter. She grabbed the roll and peeled off a long piece. She wadded it up and pressed it against the young man's wound. "Here, you do it." Roxy took the man's hand and placed it over the gash. "Keep pressure on it."

Roxy took her cell phone out of her back pocket. She punched in 9-1-1. "Hello? This is Deputy Nez with the Yucca Basin Sheriff's

Department. I'm at the Quick Stop just out of town. I have a male in his early twenties that's been stabbed. Dispatch an ambulance right away."

She looked at the young man. "Who did this?"

"Some guy. He came in and—"

Roxy heard a vehicle outside peal out on the asphalt. She looked out the front windows and saw a truck race across the front parking lot and speed onto the highway.

She looked down at the young man. "Keep pressure on it. I have to go. An ambulance is on the way."

Roxy leaped over the counter and darted out of the store. She jumped into her car and started the engine. She slammed it into reverse, did a three-quarter turn, and gunned the Chevelle onto the highway. The truck already had a quarter-mile head start so she stomped the gas pedal to the floor, letting up only to double-shift into the next gear as she thundered down the road.

Hitting ninety, Roxy held the steering wheel with one hand and put the phone up to her ear. "This is Deputy Nez. I'm following a suspect. Brown Ford pickup. Heading south on Highway 9. Officer needs assistance."

The front end shimmied from the high speed. Roxy dropped her phone on the passenger seat so she could grip the steering wheel with both hands. The truck up ahead nearly lost it when the right tires drifted onto the shoulder but the driver managed to get it back on the road.

Roxy gave it more gas and saw the speedometer creep over a hundred. "You're going to get us both killed!" she yelled at the driver in the truck.

The truck suddenly skidded to a near stop, and hung a sharp right down a dirt road into a grove of fig trees.

Roxy downshifted and pumped the brakes. She cranked the wheel. The rear tires on the Chevelle squealed as the car left the tarmac and rolled onto the dirt road.

Driving into a thick plume of dust, Roxy had to slow down.

Suddenly the tailgate of the truck came into view. Roxy stood on the brakes and the Chevy came to a stop, narrowly avoiding hitting the back of the truck. She leaned over and pushed the release on the glove compartment. The door dropped down. She reached in and grabbed her Ruger .38 revolver.

Roxy jumped out of the car and approached the side of the truck. As the dust cleared, she could see why the truck had stopped. A long-boom cherry picker had been left in the middle of the road.

"Put your hands out the window where I can see them!" Roxy shouted.

She saw the driver's window slowly crank down.

"Did you hear me? Let me see those hands!"

A hand appeared and waved, then disappeared back in the cab.

Roxy held her gun out in front of her. She stepped toward the driver's door. She could see the man in the side mirror, watching her approaching. "I'm not going to tell you again." She swiveled around and pointed her gun directly at the driver. He was a big man, scruffy looking with a thin beard. He kept staring straight ahead like he hadn't heard a word she had said.

She glanced at the passenger seat and saw a Quick Stop bag, money spilled out onto the floor mat. "Get out!" Roxy aimed her revolver at the man's head. She put her left hand on the handle, and opened the door. "Nice and slow." She placed her hand on the window frame.

The man was lightning-fast. He knocked her gun hand out of the way, and in one quick motion, stabbed her hand resting on the window frame. The blade of the hunting knife went all the way through her hand and down into the doorframe.

Roxy screamed and dropped her gun. The man shoved the door open with his shoulder. Roxy fell back onto her butt. As soon as the man was out of the truck, he kicked her in the ribs. When she yelped, he kicked her again in the hip. He bent down, picked up her gun, and tucked it in his belt.

"Stupid bitch!" He grabbed the handle of the buck knife and yanked out the blade.

With her hand free, Roxy collapsed on her back.

"Get up!" the man ordered.

Cupping her bleeding hand against her chest, Roxy said, "You might as well give it up. The police are on the way."

"What are you, a cop?"

"That's right."

"Bullshit, you don't look like a cop!" He reached down and grabbed Roxy by the hair and lifted her up onto her feet.

"Get your hands off of me!"

"Shut up!" The man punched Roxy in the face. Her knees almost buckled but she stayed on her feet. "Think you're tough, eh?" He pushed her to the ground. "Take off your clothes."

"Screw you," Roxy said defiantly.

"Do as I say." He grabbed her left boot by the heel and yanked it off.

Roxy scampered back.

"Want me to cut up that pretty face of yours?" The man showed her the pointy blade of his knife.

"What does it matter? You're going to kill me anyway."

"Might as well have a little fun. Who knows, you might like it."

"I doubt that."

"I'm not going to tell you again. Take off your damn clothes."

"All right. If that's what you want." Roxy pulled off her other boot. She took both her socks off. She removed her tank top then slipped out of her jeans. She stood up, wearing only her bra and briefs.

"I said everything!"

"I don't think so." Roxie raised her left hand. The jagged blade had left a gaping hole in the middle of her palm.

She watched the expression on the Quick Stop Killer's face steadily change from shock when he saw the punctured wound on her hand close up and the skin heal in the blink of an eye, to a look of horror when her body shapeshifted from a beautiful woman into a lycanthrope beast, and finally his look of ultimate terror when she raked her claws across his throat.

Priceless.

THE END

TO THE READER

I hope you enjoyed *CRYPTID FRONTIER*. If you like the series, you can learn more about these characters in *CRYPTID ISLAND*, the exciting prequel to *CRYPTID ZOO* and its sequel *CRYPTID COUNTRY* followed by *CRYPTID CIRCUS, CRYPTID NATION, CRYPTID KINGDOM* and this installment, *CRYPTID FRONTIER.*

ACKNOWLEDGEMENTS

I would like to thank Gary Lucas, Romana Baotic, Nichola Meaburn and the wonderful people working with Severed Press that helped with this book. It's truly amazing how folks who live in the most incredible places in the world can truly enrich our lives. A special thanks to my wonderful daughter and faithful beta reader Genene Griffiths Ortiz for her enthusiasm and making this so much fun. And of course, I would like to thank you, the reader, for taking the time to share these bizarre and incredible journeys with me.

ABOUT THE AUTHOR

Gerry Griffiths lives in San Jose, California, with his wife and their five rescue dogs and a cat. He is a Horror Writers Association member and has over thirty published short stories in various anthologies and magazines, along with a collection entitled *Creatures* and his latest novel *In Case of Carnage: A Paranormal Crime Novel*. He is also the author of *Silurid, The Beasts of Stoneclad Mountain, Death Crawlers, Deep in the Jungle, The Next World, Battleground Earth, Down From Beast Mountain, Terror Mountain, Cryptid Zoo, Cryptid Country, Cryptid Island, Cryptid Circus, Cryptid Nation, Cryptid Kingdom*, and *Cryptid Frontier.*

CHECK OUT OTHER GREAT BIGFOOT NOVELS

THE BEASTS OF STONECLAD MOUNTAIN by Gerry Griffiths

Clay Morgan is overjoyed when he is offered a place to live in a remote wilderness at the base of a notorious mountain. Locals say there are Bigfoot living high up in the dense mountainous forest. Clay is skeptic at first and thinks it's nothing more than tall tales.

But soon Clay becomes a believer when giant creatures invade his new home and snatch his baby boy, Casey.

Now, Clay and his wife, Mia, must rescue their son with the help of Clay's uncle and his dog, a journey up the foreboding mountain that will take them into an unimaginable world...straight into hell!

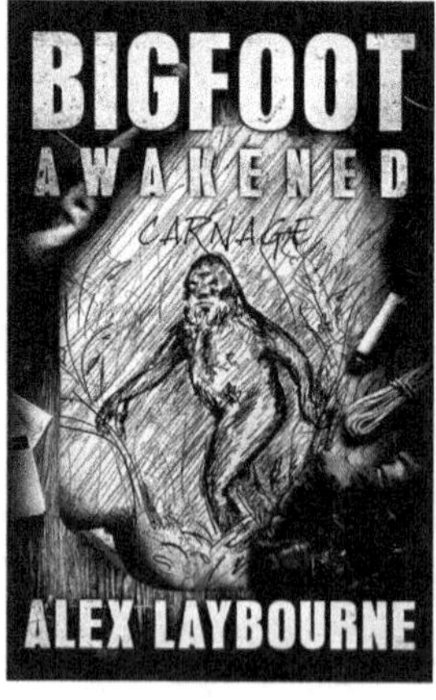

BIGFOOT AWAKENED by Alex Laybourne

A weekend away with friends was supposed to be fun. One last chance for Jamie to blow off some steam before she leaves for college, but when the group make a wrong turn, fun is the last thing they find.

From the moment they pass through a small rural town they are being hunted by whatever abominations live in the woods.

Yet, as the beasts attack and the truth is revealed, they learn that despite everything, man still remains the most terrifying evil of them all.

CHECK OUT OTHER GREAT CRYPTID NOVELS

RETURN TO DYATLOV PASS
by J.H. Moncrieff

In 1959, nine Russian students set off on a skiing expedition in the Ural Mountains. Their mutilated bodies were discovered weeks later. Their bizarre and unexplained deaths are one of the most enduring true mysteries of our time. Nearly sixty years later, podcast host Nat McPherson ventures into the same mountains with her team, determined to finally solve the mystery of the Dyatlov Pass incident. Her plans are thwarted on the first night, when two trackers from her group are brutally slaughtered. The team's guide, a superstitious man from a neighboring village, blames the killings on yetis, but no one believes him. As members of Nat's team die one by one, she must figure out if there's a murderer in their midst—or something even worse—before history repeats itself and her group becomes another casualty of the infamous Dead Mountain.

DOVER DEMON
by Hunter Shea

The Dover Demon is real...and it has returned. In 1977, Sam Brogna and his friends came upon a terrifying, alien creature on a deserted country road. What they witnessed was so bizarre, so chilling, they swore their silence. But their lives were changed forever. Decades later, the town of Dover has been hit by a massive blizzard. Sam's son, Nicky, is drawn to search for the infamous cryptid, only to disappear into the bowels of a secret underground lair. The Dover Demon is far deadlier than anyone could have believed. And there are many of them. Can Sam and his reunited friends rescue Nicky and battle a race of creatures so powerful, so sinister, that history itself has been shaped by their secretive presence?

CHECK OUT OTHER GREAT CRYPTID NOVELS

SWAMP MONSTER MASSACRE
by Hunter Shea

The swamp belongs to them. Humans are only prey. Deep in the overgrown swamps of Florida, where humans rarely dare to enter, lives a race of creatures long thought to be only the stuff of legend. They walk upright but are stronger, taller and more brutal than any man. And when a small boat of tourists, held captive by a fleeing criminal, accidentally kills one of the swamp dwellers' young, the creatures are filled with a terrifyingly human emotion—a merciless lust for vengeance that will paint the trees red with blood.

TERROR MOUNTAIN
by Gerry Griffiths

When Marcus Pike inherits his grandfather's farm and moves his family out to the country, he has no idea there's an unholy terror running rampant about the mountainous farming community. Sheriff Avery Anderson has seen the heinous carnage and the mutilated bodies. He's also seen the giant footprints left in the snow—Bigfoot tracks. Meanwhile, Cole Wagner, and his wife, Kate, are prospecting their gold claim farther up the valley, unaware of the impending dangers lurking in the woods as an early winter storm sets in. Soon the snowy countryside will run red with blood on TERROR MOUNTAIN.

www.ingramcontent.com/pod-product-compliance
Lightning Source LLC
Chambersburg PA
CBHW061240170626
46809CB00007B/2756